The Gift of an Imaginary Girl

Coco & Other Stories

The Gift of an Imaginary Girl

Coco & Other Stories

by

Kristy Webster

A Word with You Press®

Publishers and Purveyors of Fine Stories in the Digital Age
Moscow, Idaho

The Gift of an Imaginary Girl: Coco & Other Stories
is published by:
A Word with You Press®

310 East A Street, Suite B, Moscow, Idaho 83843

For information, please direct emails to:
info@awordwithyoupress.com or visit our website:
www.awordwithyoupress.com

Cover design and interior layout: Teri Rider, www.teririder.com

First Edition, October 2015
Printed in the United States of America

10 9 8 7 6 5 4 3 2 1   15 16 17 18 19 20 21 22 23 24

For my sons, Isaac & Parker.

ART Plates

Contents

Acknowledgements

First, I want to thank everyone from A Word with You Press, especially Thorn Sully, Editor-in-Chief and personal guardian angel.

A huge thanks to Tiffany Vakilian, Teri Rider, Billy Holder and Morgan Sully; without their tireless and generous contributions, this dream would not have come true for me.

I'd like to thank the members of my writing group: Tamara Sellman, Julie Leung, Kathryn Lafond and Jennifer Wilhoit, who saw the earliest drafts of many of these stories. Thanks to Therese Mancevski who was the first to read and review Coco for me.

Thank you to Lola Haskins, Wes Cecil and Bill Ransom for their mentoring.

I want to thank the women who inspired some of my characters: Soledad, Consuelo, Gollita, Antonia, Clementina, and my Abuela Magdalena, who though I never met her managed to pierce the veil and infuse my inner world with her magical presence. Thank you to my mother and father for the gift of the Spanish language.

Thank you to my siblings, Jon, Marta and Jeanie who not only contributed to the campaign to get my book published, but gave me their loving support and encouragement.

Thank you to all the friends and colleagues who infused me with enough confidence to keep going. Thank you to Peter and Anna Quinn from The Writers' Workshoppe and Imprint Books. More of the support, both financial and emotional came from my bookstore friends and community. Thank you Anna and Peter, for giving me a "home."

Most of all, thank you to my sons, Isaac and Parker Fink, the loves of my life for whom I do it all.

Foreword

Readers claim that they pick up a book in order to escape. But what of the author? Why did they pick up the pen?

Kristy Webster realized at a very young age that there was no world into which she could escape, unless she created it herself.

Often a writer believes the expression of personal pain is art; it is not. Pain is simply the array of colors on the artist's palette. What Kristy has done is to impress those paints, those words and acrylics, upon a canvas, and a metamorphosis occurred. Blood became ink, pain became passion. Agony became art.

Kristy's stories are inspiring and up-lifting, authentic and terribly intimate.

A Word with You Press is delighted that Kristy chose us to share her work and her life with you.

What follows is magic.

Thornton Sully
Editor-in-Chief
A Word With You Press
Publishers and Purveyors of Fine Stories in the Digital Age

Prologue

The Visitors

At church I struggled to pay attention. In poems, I slid my fingers through the onyx locks of Christ himself. Banshees begged to be drawn in the pages of His Word. This thing, Art, wanted me. Bad. How did I explain this to a Father who only read the Good Book?

Dogma worked its parasites deep inside my bones. I took blades to my forearms, my legs, watched the skin separate and the red beads of blood blossom.

Beneath the surface, there she was: untamed and untamable, Wolf girl, maybe even Dragon girl. I let her out only a little bit at a time in moments of secret solitude: my bedroom closet, the bathtub, the roof of my father's work-shed. There I would say as I pressed down the razor, *Breathe while you can, breath deep because who knows when you'll get this chance again.*

One night I dreamt that spirit children tapped on the glass and helped me crawl out of my bedroom window. It was dawn, the morning oozed through a filter of milky blue. The spirits asked me to dance and when I said I didn't know how, they took me by the hand and led me through tall waves of turquoise grass. We swayed to the rhythm of the field, we embodied the vibration of the moon, and sung the sun anew. The spirits promised me they were not just a dream, but visitors who made themselves known to me the only way they could.

When I awoke to spend another lonely day at school, the center of my palms pulsed and tingled. I still felt their enchanted touch.

And though I was still very much alone, a sad, trapped child, I knew to believe in my dream. I knew someday I would be a visitor, too.

Everything Is Spectacular

Consuelo tells me if she makes one more latte she will certainly kill herself. I am grateful I poured my own drip. She says on days like these all she thinks of is the little pond in her backyard filled with goldfish. She compliments me on my red skirt and when I tell her it only cost me two bucks at the Goodwill she smiles.

The man in line behind me, sports a leather briefcase and a hounds-tooth sports jacket. He's just the type of man that will order a skinny-double-tall-Irish-cream-latte.

I imagine sweeping Consuelo into my arms and carrying her off. We could dip our fingertips in the pond and watch the goldfish swim, exist, know they are goldfish or know nothing at all. Perhaps, Consuelo is one of my many mothers, and she came from the sea and the goldfish are my sisters. Maybe what she really meant when she told me about her pond is that she is a goldfish too. Beneath her olive skin she is pure gold and her human dress melts away when she touches the water. It could be I'm golden too if only I had the courage to undress.

It must be agony to be gold on the inside and surrounded by plastic all day, every day. The tapping, coughing, throat-clearing man approaches the counter. He orders two cappuccinos with his cell phone glued to his ear, never realizing how far the tide has rolled in, how close he came to getting wet.

Mothers in Trees

As a young girl Lupe stole dolls from toddlers, played pranks on her little sister, and dipped her pinky into the Holy Water.

Though she wasn't beautiful Lupe was pretty enough. More than that she was smart, talented and sassy. Boys either found her to be a hard headed little witch or an utterly enchanting girl genius. Lupe valued boys who could quote Shakespeare, or Faulkner or Hemingway, boys who knew when to capitalize, and where to put periods and semi-colons. Lupe carefully inspected love letters from would-be suitors for errors in grammar, misspellings and repetitive adjectives. She was generous with her red ink pen, crossing out obvious clichés, circling passive language. In the end she'd return the letters without a word often smoothing the stationary out before displaying it face up on a young boy's desk.

Lupe also fancied herself a spy and took it upon herself to watch the comings and goings of amorous neighbors. When she tired of spying, she took to thievery, stealing bracelets and baskets from street vendors. When spying and stealing failed to thrill her she'd find someone or something to bother and rile up. One day she decided to torture her mother's chickens. After all, she found them insignificant. They were meat on legs running and cackling obnoxiously through the dusty yard.

That day Lupe was not thinking of the nine-foot leather belt that had once belonged to her great, great grandmother Concha who they called "The Hippo." Since she could no longer fit through the door, when Concha died friends and family were forced to break down the walls of her house. It took twenty men just to lift her off the floor. But even the strongest men in the village couldn't manage to move her more than just a couple feet.

According to Lupe's mother, at least two of the men had heart attacks that day from the strain the lifting put on their bodies. Rather than risk the lives and health of the rest of the men, the movers decided to bury Concha where she fell so that her home became her catacomb. They dug a huge hole through the floor, the pavement, and the dirt, rolled Concha in, and covered her up. They stuck a cross to mark her grave. They say that the cross was buried in a tropical storm and that after a while people forgot what lay beneath the mound of dirt and someone built a slide and a swing-set there.

Concha's belt became something of an urban myth. School children insisted that as it passed from mother to daughter the belt grew even longer, thicker. So when Lupe, who was chasing a flock of terrified chickens, heard the belt cutting through air she dropped the mango she had in her right hand, ready to throw at one of the slower hens. The leather hit her spine like a jagged string of teeth. Hard as she tried not to give her mother the satisfaction, she couldn't help but wail and collapse face first, where she met the hens at eye level.

"Your punishment is this," her mother started, "I'm going to the market. It shouldn't take me more than two hours. You like to terrorize these hens, Lupe, no? Pues, I have a job for you. Catch one of these," she pointed at one cluster, "and cut her head off. Then pluck the feathers off her body, cut her again and pull out all her guts. Then, you cook her. When I get home I want to see the feast on the table. ¡Para que te da pena!"

The thought of touching a dirty chicken let alone feeling its warm blood splash her face, was worse than the promise of a whipping. As soon as Lupe's mother's wide, dark figure turned its back and walked away Lupe did what she did best in moments like this. She climbed the mango tree.

It's not that the belt couldn't have reached her. It's that Lupe's mother loved that tree. Lupe had positioned herself thoughtfully so that branches strewn with mangos enveloped her at every angle. Lupe's mother didn't dare risk bruising and knocking down the mangos. Instead she would wait for a heavy rain to flush Lupe out, or hunger, or loneliness.

"This time," Lupe's mother said, "When I whip you, the belt will wrap around your arms and legs so you can never climb my tree again."

With the chicken chaser up in the tree the hens were free to "bawk-bawk" and parade around the yard without fear. That is when the rooster cut through the assembled hens like Moses parting the red sea, approaching the tree with great pomp and purpose.

It turned out, the rooster was a poet. He scratched words in the dirt that melted Lupe's milk chocolate skin. He knew the precise placement of the comma, the difference between "your" and "you're." Even his penmanship was impeccable. Lupe read his words out loud and when she did the rooster did a little dance, as though he were worshipping her.

Lupe's mother would be home in less than half an hour, and what would she find, but Lupe enamored with the literary genius of a rooster. Even with minutes to spare, Lupe imagined the belt coming at her like a skinny dragon with all its teeth on fire. But as long as she stayed in the tree, she could not know for sure if the rooster was a poet taking the form of a rooster, or a rooster posing as a poet.

Finally, Lupe decided it was time one way or the other to face her fate. She climbed down with her back to the rooster. Her smile was taking over her face and she felt no girl should flatter a rooster with such blatant adoration. She turned coquettishly and walked towards the rooster like a muse. It was because of such a state that it came as such a shock to her when she felt a sharp peck at her heel. She turned looked down and saw a testy little hen. When the rooster tilted his body to get a better look at the hen, Lupe could see she was no longer the center of his universe.

When her mother arrived home from the market, Lupe was still plucking the last feathers from the limp, headless body, her legs covered in red dust and trampled poetry.

The Goods

In the end you want someone not fancy or even clean, but someone good. He has to always say things he absolutely means, he has to do the things that prove the words he has spoken to you not once, but always and again, and again. To be good means he doesn't forget how to love you when you make him suffer. It means he will not let the old woman on the bus stand and wobble in the wake of every sharp turn. He will be good, he will say, Please ma'am, take my seat. If the dog is too sick to eat, to move, to even breathe, he will not hesitate, he will be good and in all that goodness, even as he buries that poor dog he will keep saying, You were a good dog, the best dog ever. When humans die he will not bring over a casserole or tell them how sorry he is for their loss, he won't use words at a time when words cruelly chew up newer ghosts. He will use his eyes and his hands; he will place a hand on a shoulder or the top of a head. He will absorb the grief; he will drive it into his bones and release it through his own tears, out into the world where the grief can breathe again, where it will find a dark kind of love.

He will touch you when you want to be touched and let you be when your hackles rise. He will be good to you, resist the urge to shackle you in guilt. He will be good in the way that he listens, because he will hear not just the things you say but the notes beneath their sounds too, and understand the very essence of its meaning.

He will be too good and you will go looking for pain like you always do. You'll find pain, you'll marinate inside its stale waters, its blackened pools. You'll go so numb you will forget to even feel ashamed. You'll believe that pain is good for you. You will trouble yourself with finding new kinds of pain. You will trouble yourself.

You will remember the good you haven't found; the good that never came. The dream of that goodness rises in blue steam from the back of your neck. Your pain has been disassembled, liquefied and turned to vapors, gases that suffocate the memory of a phantom goodness.

In the end, you will want someone good. But you will choose the jagged edge of a broken rock over the smoothness of a round, naked stone. You will suffer because you believe you have to. You will choose building strength over finding peace.

Birth

A woman was in the habit of taking on lovers and not repeating herself. At night, upon their arrival she would open the door to her home without a word, turn and walk away, letting her silky cape fall to the floor, leaving a trail for the man in the doorway. In the dark, her body was a collection of moons. In the morning she would offer coffee, and leave all conversation to her paramour, while keeping herself in little books, secretly stacked inside her ribs.

One lover wanted the library of her. This was a tricky business. He had to fool her with countless disguises so she wouldn't tire of him. Every time he came to her, he was a new man. He paid attention to what endeared her to his many faces, until he knew how to put them together into one man. One night, he decided his collage was complete, and while she slept, he cut out a diamond-shaped piece of her skin below her belly button. He ate the flesh to keep part of her inside of him, assuming this was the way.

When she awoke, he told her, "There will be no more others." She smiled, because in truth, this woman wanted someone to put an end to her dizzying, addictive lust.

The man could see in the woman's eyes her catalog of lovers, years of men who shared her bed, her body, and it drove him mad. He set her bed on fire. That's how it started. He would say, "Show me where else they've been in your house."

She pointed to the couch, the kitchen counter, the hallway, and the oval-shaped rug now pale and weary from the friction of bodies. She touched the bookshelves, the windowsills, the shower, the garden, the table, and the chairs surrounding the table. "Here, here, here."

"The whole house then," he said, and lit the match.

The house burned like paper, its flaming edges floating up to the sky like the ghosts of old women. Even her black cape disappeared in the smoke.

This, however, was not enough. The man demanded to know every place on her body she'd ever been touched. She surrendered to his examination. He left her naked on the grass and returned with pen and ink to mark every part of her with his name. If the ink smeared, he traced his name over and over again, each time pressing harder.

Weeks later the woman felt a shy, low trembling inside of her and announced it to the man. She likened it to dancing moths.

He kept the woman in a tree after this, so no one else could reach her. He brought her peaches and raisins, sometimes biscuits. Every night he slept at the bottom of the tree, resting upon its trunk. Some nights, he dreamt the woman grew wings, and this terrified him. In the morning, he would look up at her skinny brown arms and feel at peace again.

As the woman's belly grew, the man saw the places where he'd written his name grow as well. How big a part of her he'd become. When it came time for the child to be born the man took the woman to the beach. He promised a bed in the middle of the ocean, a cradle made from pearl, shark meat and clams for dinner, promised sealskin, cut and sewn to her flesh, where a part of her was missing.

The woman only half listened. With every contraction, her body became less and less hers, more belonging to the earth, more to the tree which had been her home for all those months. She looked down at her spread legs, and thought she saw beastly branches and coarse leaves. She closed her eyes and thought about her silky black cape, the last garment of her old life. She remembered its ashes floating on the sky like blackened moths and somehow the pain produced by this memory dulled the pain of the bearing down, the tremendous pressure.

As the woman howled, the man grew sick with anticipation, anxious to see his face atop a small, slippery body. Instead, what emerged from his round house of a woman was a full-grown, naked man, the first of many past lovers she was yet to give birth to. The woman shook her head. She dug her hands in the sand, deep, as if searching for an explanation that didn't exist.

"Whore," he said, and left her screaming, left her to her hairy, clumsy children.

The man had walked several miles before he felt the tiny explosions going off inside him, and how he regretted the part of her he'd swallowed, the diamond of her body he could not give back.

The Message

A young woman had a son but no husband. She worked as a maid scrubbing caked mud off lobby floors. She picked up wrappers left behind by children. She carried two buckets of water at a time, up six flights of stairs. Her black hair turned white and straw-like in just a few years. The skin on her hands turned so translucent you could see the blood pulsing beneath the surface. The woman's body aged so much that passersby believed she was the boy's grandmother.

The woman worked herself into an old lady so her son could go to college. She imagined him as a doctor, a business man, a school teacher. She imagined him never immersing his hands in buckets full of Clorox Bleach and hot water. Never scraping gum from under tables, never eating slices of orange off the floor left behind by hurried crowds.

When the boy became a man the mother took out a schoolbook from many years ago that she never learned how to read. Inside, she had carved a space where she had stashed the money she'd bled for all these years.

"This is for your dreams," the mother told him, with tears in her eyes.

He grabbed a few bills from the top, to make sure they were real.

"My dream," he told her, "is to wander the world, on my own, with nothing but the shirt on my back and the hat on my head. My dream is to dig my hands in the dirt and make my own way. My dream is to walk circles around the world, until one day I find my father. Then I will rest."

The son put the bills back. He closed the book. He kissed his mother on the cheek and walked out the door.

The woman threw the cash in the stove. She collapsed and cried so hard, her tears flooded the kitchen floor. The empty book floated to the surface. The woman reached out just before going under. Her wrinkled hand fit the carved out space as if the two were made for each other. Black letters appeared on her fingers and palms, grew into sentences, then paragraphs, and lastly, pages. She still couldn't read the words. She didn't need to.

Dream Dog

These kisses happen in my dreams with men I haven't met, who maybe don't exist at all. Last night while kissing one of these men our bodies joined at the lips but the rest of our bodies disassembled—a leg floated out the window, a buttocks and a torso rolled into the backseat. Our mouths sucked so hard eventually that was all that was left, just our lips and teeth and tongues as the rest of us disappeared. We did not miss our other parts.

I have been looking for a dog. Before the kissing dreams, I had dog dreams. Like the men, the dog may or may not exist. But I dreamed so many dreams about that same dog I am convinced the dog not only exists, but the dog is calling me. I've scoured Craigslist.org logging several hours at work a day. I am looking for a dog on the edge of human, a dog who wants to speak, a dog who knows I am the only one.

Cats moan outside my window while the computer screen echoes off my face, my tired eyes. Dogs consume me. Not only my dog, my dream dog, but after hundreds of hours of searching, I feel all dogs are calling me. I can't, I whisper, I can't take you all.

This time I cry before the man kisses me because he is so tender. We are enveloped by a warm sphere of light, the bed unfamiliar and soft. He tells me I write what I'm too afraid to speak out loud. A dog barks. A new light wakes me. My face has yet to dry.

Four dogs stare up at me, heads tilted, wondering how I manage--so bald, so raw and open. I want so much. All they want is to be fed.

All four dogs are ones I was once convinced were my dream dog. But once I brought them home, once I let them on my bed or fed them scraps from my take-out boxes, I came to realize, they were not it. I have found my dogs in overcrowded shelters, Craigslist ads--MOVING CAN'T TAKE SCRAPPY WITH— even tied to fence posts with signs reading "FREE", but nothing is free, not even love. Most of all love. Let alone dreams.

It happens the first night of my period. A howl. The dirt smells richer when I bleed. The nights are restless, sometimes the tears are unstoppable and not even the embarrassments of late night talk shows drown them out. The howl is more primal than that of a dog. The howl grows stronger and closer and I know. I understand. But curled up in sheets, soaked with red, my fear is hot and scorching. I don't answer the door. I can't answer the call.

A neighborhood child I've always found bothersome is wailing. I cover my gory scene in a fat robe and wander out, half dazed. The mother grabs her child, forces his wet face against her breasts. A dog is dead. Demolished by a careless driver. The dog lays bloody in the middle of the road. My dream dog murdered because of my fear. I am a careless dreamer.

This kiss is just as potent but less tender. The teeth are ruthless, the tongue is dangerous and weird. Black. Cold. I wake up mid climax, my four dogs, whining by the bed. They only want to be fed.

Graduation

The Doctor who fixed Maria's madness was nearly impossible to look at. Not because she was ugly, but because she was so severely handsome. Her face and body were arranged in sharp angles that sliced the air as she moved through space. When the Doctor sat in her armchair, Maria wondered if the cushions cried out when the daggers of her elbows sunk into them.

Once healed, Maria's Doctor opened her arms, revealing the barbwire bridge of veins leading to her frozen chest. As Maria approached, she noticed the Doctor's eyes for the first time, gray planets blurred by milky steam, full of memories, of things that aren't supposed to happen, but quite often do. When the Doctor's patients graduate, they say they wouldn't change a thing, wouldn't be who they are without the curling iron, the fists, the closets, the torn nylons, the china, the snow, the father, the mother, the brother the sister, at least, that's what they say.

The embrace might grant them each a gift. For Maria, this might cauterize the mended places in her mind. For the Doctor, it might offer the gift of softness that only a human touch can. Maria pressed her doughy body into the Doctor's jagged rock one.

They say that when the Doctor shattered, her cells broke into shards of stone and scattered throughout neighborhood gardens. The stones held down the roots of daffodils and tulips until the rains came and pushed them into the earth, like hard pillows for earthworms and ants. They say the stones are still listening to whispers of damage. They say Maria kept three, the same ones she let slip away while she was still broken.

The Mother Song

The man returned to his wife after seven months. He'd left to find himself and locate the love he'd lost for her, but by then, it was too late.

The wife had taken her two boys, one on her back, one by the hand, and returned to her father's country. There she ate potatoes and shellfish by the sea. Her aunts and uncles fed her legacies and legends, infused her and made her whole again with tales of her ancestors.

When the man returned to their empty home, he covered the walls in letters of apology, words that told of his regrets and promised her a life of comfort, the dream of a model husband who'd learned his lesson.

But the wife had shorn the hair from her head and forgotten her husband's touch. The wife bled every month and made herself tea. Wife became Woman, and gathered her children onto her lap and sung them the songs of her father, told them how once her people spoke the language of both beasts and angels alike.

The husband sought out his wife to make a home of her like before. But upon finding her, she offered him the only gift she had left for him: a jar filled with the sand where she'd slept alongside her sons during his absence.

When the man opened the jar, pain escaped. He found himself in those grains, those miniscule but terrifying little worlds.

The Leaving

The danger in being touched by such a gentle and confident ghost was that she'd fear death even less. But because she was more alone than she could possibly bear, she called to him by name and he responded by lifting her up inside the dark air of her room. She closed her eyes, and let her entire body relax as she levitated off the floor. The ghost spun her in the air like a seasoned dance partner. Before long, the other world called to him to return. Softly, in his arms she descended and touched the cold floor again. When he disappeared, she was left with a fresh sort of sadness that after a few days felt like love.

Brothers

She said that the nectarine she bit into tasted like jazz, like Friday nights. This was the last straw for Solomon. But he couldn't tell her that he stopped loving her on account of her turning everything into poetry. He couldn't tell her that he'd grown to despise her beginning with the time she likened his melting ice cream cone to the flooding of a silky moon. It was after all, Rocky Road–for Christ's sake–and he'd been sitting in the sun with her for a good hour listening to her go on and on about the sparrows, and the light and the shadows, and didn't everything have its own song, its own harmony, its own inescapable destiny? All he wanted was to eat his ice cream. But he couldn't tell her that he'd lost all passion for her because of her lyricism.

"Too bad your lips look like that I might have loved you." With that he got up, bit into a crisp, green apple and walked away, leaving the girl to her metaphors, her seamless poetry. He strolled along and as he witnessed the day, the ugly men and women, the tedious children, the skinny, barking dogs, he smiled. He attached no meaning to their existence. There they were, there it was, and that was all.

When he came home to the house he shared with his brother, Jacob, he asked for potatoes. His younger brother did all the cooking, as he never left the house. At age sixteen Jacob came home in a state of madness saying only that he'd "seen too much of the world" and was never going out again. He said if he were to go out again, he would surely drop dead—on account of the pressure of the sky on his shoulders, the cracks in the sidewalk, the endless doors and their terrible houses. So Solomon supported the two of them with his little paper route and the errands he ran for Mrs.

Puckett: Mrs. Puckett who at age seventy-five, never gave up trying to seduce Solomon, Mrs. Puckett who wore her heels to bed and drank whiskey (in Earl Grey tea) in the back of Solomon's car on the way to her hair appointments. Still, what Mrs. Puckett gave paid for potatoes and cigarettes.

"I ended things with that wordy girl," Solomon announced, "I don't want a book. I want a woman."

Jacob wanted to understand his brother. He offered him more leeks. Jacob had heard of this girl for months now. Having never seen her, he had no choice but create his own portrait of her. He imagined a girl with brown curls, like his mother had before she married his angry father. He imagined her conversing in poems on a park bench, never looking in one particular direction, but always somewhere upwards, her eyes never focusing on anything tangible, anything obvious. He imagined her pages suspended in sky.

"If she comes here looking for me," Solomon told his brother, "Get rid of her."

Several weeks passed and the girl did not come. In that time Mrs. Puckett had twice tried to get Solomon to undress her, saying her arthritis was acting up, and she couldn't possibly tug at the zipper like that, her wrists would surely snap from the pressure. In that same time, Jacob had swept the floor fifty-three times, he'd cooked well over one hundred potatoes, he'd waited all day, every day, for his brother's return, a way to taste and smell the world, without letting the world taste and smell him. Jacob could never tell anyone what happened to him that one day when he was sixteen. That day, he went out, looked around, and everything he saw was skinless. That is to say, all the filters on the living had vanished. He'd become accustomed to seeing people as walking puzzles, but on that day, there was a moment when the pieces came together. No one was a mystery. That day, people were made of glass. A crumpled old man, bent down to pick up his donut—it had fallen as he juggled it with a newspaper and coffee. A goat-faced boy snatched it before the old man could reach it. He stuffed it into his mouth all at once and ran—his blue shorts a flag showcasing his ornery success. The old man sobbed openly on the sidewalk. Jacob stood close enough to hear the glass shatter.

In his celibacy and in the absence of a wordy woman, Solomon grew fond of Mrs. Puckett in unexpected ways. Maybe it was because they drank tea in silence—no commentary about what it felt like to drink the tea, mind you, just the drinking of it alone. Maybe it was because her little blue eyes disappeared when she smiled each time Solomon opened her car door, letting her out onto that same sidewalk his brother Jacob feared so fervently.

Solomon thought he'd tell Mrs. Puckett that she had finally won. But upon arriving at her door, he found that he wanted to tell her much more and what he had not counted on was the urge to give Mrs. Puckett a description of her victory, a comparison of her with something else, and he found himself lonely for that irritating girl's way with words.

Jacob was not accustomed to opening the door of his own home. But someone was knocking as if her very life depended on it. Upon opening the door, a sorry looking girl with flat brown curls, a girl who'd sewn her lips together—resembling a seam binding two quilt squares—stood before him, holding out an envelope, addressed: For Solomon. In the young girl's eyes, Jacob saw painstaking words threaded together in a sea of books and he too, felt himself drowning. The girl left Jacob to that familiar misery, and floated away, the sidewalk devouring each one of her steps.

At a loss for words, Solomon left Mrs. Puckett with daisies and an open door. He returned home to find his own door stuttering, the door not knowing which way it should swing. He noticed the envelope with his name on it. Inside, a note asked, "And now?"

"Where is she? Where is she, Jacob?" Solomon searched the house desperate for either one of them. But the house was like a vacuum and he felt the hostile air surround him with its cold fingers. In his hand, the note, the words rubbing off inside his sweaty palm.

"Jacob!"

But Jacob had walked out barefoot, ventured into that sickening street, trembling. He'd braved the open mouth of the city, hoping the girl's pages would lead the way, hoping they would carry him off his feet.

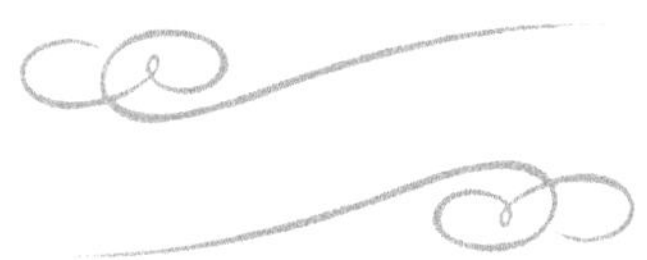

The Sisters

Big Sister walked and Little Sister floated. Passerby watched a scowling, lanky girl dressed in blue dragging a limp, white, kite behind her. Little Sister wore white on account of Mother telling her she was a gift from Heaven.

Big Sister grew sick of how Mother would ask Little Sister, "Why are you so, so sweet? How does it come so easy for you to be such an angel?" Big Sister became incensed with Little Sister's dim-witted smile, and the horrible sound of the wet kisses Little Sister would plant Mother's cheek.

On one of their walks Big Sister pointed out a dead blue jay in the street's gutter. The bird's chest had deflated like a squashed peach. The eyes hollowed out, the legs bent and twisted so they resembled question marks.

"See that?" Big Sister pointed, "Heaven is filled with them. Hundreds and thousands of things just like that."

Little Sister let go of Big Sister's hand. To passersby it appeared as though the breeze had abandoned the kite, leaving it lost in its awkward back and forth dance.

When Mother died someone stuffed her into a coffin, dressed her in a green and black floral print polyester dress. This was not Mother's loveliest dress by any stretch of the imagination. But someone had decided it was. Someone had also decided Mother looked too dead for her own funeral and had painted her face with dark rouge, so that Mother resembled a frightening, mad, old woman.

Looking at Mother inside that rectangle box Little Sister remembered Big Sister's words from years before. "Heaven is filled with them."

The Sisters hosted the wake like parallel statues never turning to look at one another until finally, Big Sister cut off a piece of pink frosted cake and offered it to Little Sister, to which she shook her head, No.

The Sisters old ladies now live on opposite sides of the same town and every time they meet on the street Big Sister says, "Hello. How are you?" Little Sister says, "Very well." "That's good," says Big Sister and Little Sister walks away.

The next time they meet Big Sister says, "Hello. How are you?" Little Sister responds the same as usual. But this time Big Sister says, "Why have you never asked me, 'How are you?' In all these years …"

"Haven't I? I thought I had."

Little Sister looks down at the oil in the gutter, she watches the swirls of green and blue, how they curve around one another without ever touching.

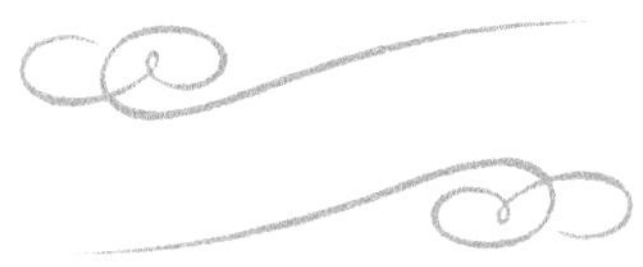

I Once Knew

1.
The Shadow

I once knew a woman with no arms who fell in love with a man who had no legs. The shadow of their naked embrace resembled a spider. He boiled her noodles cooked al dente, how she preferred them. She carried him on her back so he could see the sunset from their porch. When he died, her body started to absorb her legs until they shrunk up inside of her. Her head absorbed what was left of the body until it too, disappeared. When the memory of her love came for her head, it melted her eyes like frozen stars, drowned every last speck of silver from her hair. All but the shadow of the two of them made whole remained.

2.
The Dream

I once knew a Dream who had no idea she was a Dream. She lifted the top of our heads and dipped her toes inside our slick brains. She gently carved into our heads an alphabet of images, some grainy, some sharp and muscular. Each morning our waking destroyed her, but in our sleep she rose again, forgetting what her fevers and floats had left behind, clueless of her repetition. Until one night inside one of our minds she stayed trapped, the images collapsing upon her. Night after night, she apologizes for the death of all other dreams to that tortured dreamer.

3.
The Artist

I once knew a girl afraid of her own breasts. To overcome her fear, she began painting with them. She'd paint the nipple one color, and the rest of her breast indefinable patterns of her own making. Her paintings quickly became the talk of the art class. Though her bare breasts still frightened her, she loved how when she pressed her paint stained bosom to the canvas, paper, or wood, they resembled wildflowers, and sunflowers, a bright and thirsty garden.

Luz

That morning at the first signal of rusty blood, Lucinda decided she wouldn't bleed again. She knew at that moment she absolutely, positively, without a doubt in the world must become pregnant, must give birth, must become a mother. And although she had no home and no man to call a home, even though she had no self to self-improve, even though Lucinda was weightless, really, kind of floating in the world, she believed she had to fill her womb immediately. In fact, the hunger in her womb was so deep and desperate it took over her whole body. The hunger in her belly felt petty. The emptiness of her womb gnawed at her, it growled, it begged, FEED ME!

Because Lucinda couldn't breathe on her own she carried an oxygen mask to wear around the city. With the mask pressed over her mouth and wearing the thin veil of a pillow case turned dress Lucinda went out to find someone to fill her restless womb. She didn't find one or two but twenty. She laid with each one, quietly, without warmth, without pleasure, but with hunger, always deep and non-abating hunger. All the time, she kept the mask over her face. Once she was sure the deed had been done, Lucinda went in search of a cave in which to hibernate and just wait for everything to happen to her that was going to happen. Maybe she would die of starvation or from lack of oxygen. Maybe she'd be discovered breathless and bloated in her pillowcase dress. It could end that way. She hoped, instead she'd find a place that could hold her. After all, she didn't take up much space at all. She required little. Maybe, she even required nothing, except the air she drank from her plastic mask.

Lucinda found a hole and climbed down the hole with her mask and her oxygen. She'd become accustomed to the dark, and to the wet pressure of the dirt walls. Life was joyless, but it was life. She was breathing after all. As her belly swelled larger and larger over the next nine months, climbing in and out of the hole became a chore. So when the days grew close to delivery, she grabbed all the air she could, along with some tea and soda and went down into the hole for good. She would deliver that which would finally complete her and bring her joy in the bowels of an angry park where there were no children, only more joyless survivors kicking garbage cans and yelling at trees.

One morning Lucinda looked up at the light from the bottom of the hole and knew it was time. She felt the first contraction, not just inside her body, but also around her, squeezing her. When it was time, she pushed, all the time with her mask pressed up to her face so tight it was like second skin, a secondary feature of misery. But when Lucinda pushed, it wasn't just the life inside her that moved, it was the walls around her, and though she couldn't be certain with all the delirious pain, she believed the light was getting bigger and brighter, and that she too was being pushed up and out of the hole with every contraction, with every push.

Finally, Lucinda reached the terrifying stage of labor that would either bear great fruits or rip her in two and destroy her; the Ring of Fire, the last effort to meet with either life or death. But just as she prepared to bear down for the last time, the mask fell from her face and when she tried desperately to reach for it, she noticed that her arms, her shoulders, were pinned inside the hole in the earth, and that the walls of dirt and rock had indeed all but swallowed her whole. She moved her toes, and there was no ground beneath her. She looked up and the light was white, blinding, pulsing…She tried to breathe, but the walls around her contracted, squeezing her so hard she thought her bones were breaking, stealing whatever oxygen she had left. As she took her last breath, the light emerged at its fullest and most invasive, and in an instance, all turned to black.

The first cry filled Lucinda's lungs, turned her wet, muddied, skin pink, and her pillow case dress peeled off like expired skin. Each breath filled her belly, set her cells on fire. The white room was filled with lights, little mechanical torches, cold instruments, and voices. One voice she heard more clearly than any other. A word tiptoed across her tongue. But no language could lose itself from Lucinda's throat, only a cry, the desperate and pitiful cry of a newborn child was set free. Second by second, Lucinda was forgetting. Forgetting where she'd been, forgetting her age, her illnesses, her fears, her memories no matter how traumatic or powerful or obvious. She kept on forgetting until she even forgot her name, her descent into the dark hole, the park, the mask, the oxygen, the suffocating. The forgetting calmed her cries, and the soft, clear voice guided her, pressed Lucinda's tiny mouth to her mother's breast and fed her, her first taste of freedom.

She Wolf

Evie's mother refused to teach her how to use a sewing machine. She told her, "Evie, you might let the thread tangle. You might undo good work and replace it with not so good work. You might press the foot pedal too hard. Even worse, you might catch your fingers in the machine. That would be awful, wouldn't it? To sew over your hand?" The "mights" grew mightier and mightier.

This meant Evie had to sew by hand. She started with doll clothes, and little pillows made from scraps of outgrown slips. Any risks would float up to the ceiling like iridescent bubbles.

Evie's father refused to teach her how to mow the lawn. "You might run the mower over your mother's flower bed. You could destroy her lilacs, her daffodils, her tulips. Your mother would be so upset. You might hit a rock and the rock could ricochet into your eye. Worse yet, you might run the mower over your own foot. Think, all the bad things that could happen. How awful!"

Evie watched her brother mow the lawn on Tuesday afternoons when he didn't have soccer practice. She was still sewing but now she sewed dolls in bed. The dolls were made from old socks and they all looked like Evie. Evie had not done this on purpose.

Evie learned to draw and she didn't draw horses. She drew sad, naked women. She drew men without faces. She started with graphite, and later she learned about charcoal. The great thing about charcoal is that it blends and smears. Say you wanted to watch one those sad, naked women through a window, and stare into her tragic gray eyes. You could smear the charcoal lines of the windowsill and use your finger to plant diagonal streaks across the glass. That way the woman could remain a mystery. This means someone might be intrigued and ask you about it.

Evie's high school art teacher asked Evie if she wanted to learn how to paint. That's when the "mights" came back. Because, imagine, what happens when you think you can paint but you really can't. Think about what might happen if you splattered paint, accidentally, on someone else's shoes. At first she might say, "No biggie." But you'd know in the weeks to come that it really was a biggie because she'd pretend to not see you in the cafeteria and when she did make eye contact, she'd immediately whisper something to the student standing near them.

No. Charcoal is good. What you don't want them to see you can just smear.

The curly-haired guy she slept with kept asking, "Do you want to be my girl?"

Evie lied and said Yes. But the window was open and she snuck out before sunrise.

Before she left, she wrote him a note and stuck it on his dresser. The drawers of the dresser were plastered with stickers. You'd think he'd be shy about all those gold fire department stickers and the one of the Mystery Mobile. Maybe this had been his dresser since he was in third grade. Maybe this piece of childhood furniture reminded him of something really great, something he couldn't bear to forget. She doubted it though. People don't keep things that long. Goodwill, that's it. It's probably from Goodwill.

The note she left the guy had a phone number on it, but it wasn't Evie's. That is, by one number it wasn't. The last digit of her phone number is six, not nine. He might try that though. He might get it right just by guessing, and then he might ask, "Well are you my girl?" His dog barked as she climbed out the window. The dog, a black and white Australian Shepherd with a stolen face.

"Guess what?" Evie asked the Mystery Mobile boy.

"What?"

"I'm leaving you for someone who understands me."

So Evie left and when she did she took her dream journal with her.

This other man could decipher dreams and most times he'd tell her that all her dreams were about sex. At first she believed him, but more and more it depressed her. She once had a dream that she was in charge of caring for a great number of phoenixes and Evie thought this was one dream that he couldn't say was about sex. Not possibly.

"Well," he told her, "really, there is only one Phoenix, not a whole bunch."

"So?"

"But it's still an important dream. It means you rise above bad things." He told her.

He could have said she "transcended great difficulties." Did he actually believe Evie wasn't smart enough to get a word like "transcend"? He might have mentioned it to some of his college friends later, like, to mock her, to make fun of her. It might not be so bad to be with someone who doesn't understand you. But this guy, he left no windows open because he was always so cold. Evie thought this was because he was too thin and had nothing to insulate his flat body.

The only thing left to do was to claw, bark and bite, until, finally, he begs her to leave. And finally, he did.

The great thing lying is that people believe you. Evie especially enjoyed lying about her name. She'd always had an attachment to the name Maria. She loved how when she introduced herself to strangers, she could see the relief on their faces when they heard something familiar. Maria like the mother of God, or Maria from Westside Story. Sometimes she'd go overboard and say her name was Persephone or Antigone. Still, people believed that, and she liked it.

The bad thing about being a liar is trying to remember what lies you've told and whom you told the lies to. That's not so easy. For example if person A meets person B and they are both talking about Evie but one of them calls her Maria, and the other calls her Antigone, they might get a clue and think Evie wasn't really such hot stuff after all. That might mean Evie would have to stop lying, and that'd be too bad, because she really, really enjoyed herself.

Sometimes though, when you're kissing some hot man on the sidewalk and it's pouring down rain like in that ending scene in Breakfast at Tiffany's, sometimes it's not so romantic and it's better to tell the truth. It's better to say, "I don't like this. I'm cold."

The great thing about being gone is you never have to explain why you left. Sure, someone might look for you and actually find you, but then you could act like it's been so long, you don't recognize his face. Wouldn't they feel embarrassed? Probably, he would forget you and buy his milk and cigarettes and that'd be the end of it.

The bad thing about leaving is you might not ever hear about how some people miss you. That is, if you do the kind of leaving that you are still alive afterwards. Some people don't do it like that, so what does it matter? But if you're still around somewhere other than where those people live, you might wish you knew if they were talking about you and wondering where you went. It might be, no one cares and wouldn't that be awful? If you thought it was so important to leave, and then, come to find out, nobody cared anyway? Then you might want to do the other kind of leaving.

Evie likes fishing, almost as much as she likes lying. Her father never taught her to fish, on account of she might put a fishhook through her hand, or fall into the water, she might drown and trout would nibble off chunks of her skin. Someone would eventually find her, some old fisherman maybe, and wouldn't that be awful? A poor old fisherman finding a half-eaten girl at the bottom of the river?

This isn't the case though. When Evie goes fishing, she might catch a fish, she might not. She might fall into the water and if she did, she'd swim back to her boat. She might watch the ripples in the water and see Persephone, Antigone, Maria or, she might see the woman in the window, behind the smeared charcoal.

The Late Bloomer

Maggie played keyboard and sang at local farmers markets on Saturdays and sometimes at coffee shops. She stood out for a girl her age because she didn't wear tight jeans and glittery t-shirts. She kept her raven colored hair in chin length ringlets. She wore dresses that were fitted and lovely, modest and nostalgic, dresses that reminded older people of softer times. She carried an air much bigger, broader than her generation did collectively. She appeared sweet, but thick with purpose.

The first time Abby noticed Maggie, Maggie was singing and playing during the 4th of July. Abby handed her a twenty dollar bill for her homemade C.D. and when Maggie reached for her coin purse, Abby insisted "No, keep the change. Try some of that strawberry-rhubarb pie in the next booth." After her next set Maggie did just that. She never thought of Abby while eating the pie. She thought of strawberries and sun and butter. She contemplated the strange carved out clouds that hovered over the town, threatening to cut short the outdoor celebration. But she did not think of Abby.

Abby listened to Maggie's CD's twenty times the first day. She thought of Maggie every day. Thoughts of Maggie lead to thoughts of youth and sex but mostly youth. Nostalgia set in among those thoughts and bit the insides of her belly. She had very little rummaging to do to find the picture she ached for. It was pressed between the pages of her copy of The Little Prince. A picture of a petite little boy dressed in overalls two sizes too small, a bearded man with his hand on the little boy's shoulder, a Gothic looking and skinny woman with her hands clasped together at her waist. The photo elicited no sighs of joy, but it worked. The gnawing in her belly had stopped.

A few months after their meeting during 4th of July Maggie left Glory Town to attend her first year of college where she majored in Music and English. Maggie was the sweetheart of her family. Though she had two siblings, and older brother and older sister whom could have easily succumbed to jealousy and envy they too adored Maggie. Maggie and her smart green eyes, her snow white skin, Maggie who could sing the rage right out of the world with her sweet voice, replacing it with lightheaded ease and welcomed confusion.

During her freshman year she had her fleshy moments with boys. Usually they were clumsy, half-eaten moments. The boys were just that, boys. They poked and prodded, nibbled and teased at her places like she was a puzzle. As if once they figured her out, they would reap the reward. After several laughable missteps and fumbles, Maggie poured the rest of her half-scored virginity into her music. The songs she composed--fueled by all the sensations her body had yet to feel--were both a masterpiece and a refuge.

When Maggie returned home for the summer, she held her ukulele to her body like a second set of ribs. She closed the gap with her before-college-friends and together they formed a trio: Maggie the retro, doll-faced songstress, her best friend Yula the keyboard playing, chain smoking vegan and lastly, Saul, the cello playing math major who'd lost his virginity to Yula in the 8th grade. Together they painted and photocopied posters and plastered them throughout Glory Town's small streets, its moody alleyways.

When Abby spotted the poster in the coffee shop bulletin board announcing Maggie's local show, her face and her whole pelvic region went hot. But as she caught her reflection in window she was reminded of something one of her husband had said. He'd compared Abby to a retired race-horse, a creature once shiny and fast, who gave up speed and glamour for early comfort and undeserved softness. In her reflection, she saw thirty-six, the number of her years on this planet, distorted by the weight of those years, so that that the three and the six changed places. She'd kept a lean, boney figure most her life, but her breasts were too large for her frame, so they sagged and caused her back to curve and her shoulders to hunch forward. She'd let her hair grow uncut for years, a way to measure what the years had dealt her. Her golden brown hair lost luster and shine, and gray and white hair poked from her skull like silver shards.

That night she took scissors to her hair. As she cut closer and closer to her skull she felt her scalp breathe for the first time in years. She washed her hair with henna and noticed how the red tones warmed her skin tone. The rosewater she splashed on her face re-energized her complexion. Lastly, with a blue pencil she lined her hazel eyes, and for the first time in two decades, she saw the person she'd left behind.

Her body was her body, nothing more, nothing less. It wasn't gruesome or breathtaking, or any indication of what she had to offer. Her body held her up, enabled her to walk through the world sometimes with undesired visibility, with much more accountability than she'd ever asked for.

She skipped undergarments and went straight to her new Value Village ensemble: tight women's trousers, black and high-waisted, with wide legs that fell past her ankles. Over her breasts she wore a men's racer back tank top and over that, white pinstriped vest and a string of round, red beads. She glided her fingertip over a stem of red rouge and drew a singular line across her lips.

Everything about Maggie appeared effortless. From her kindness and charm to her talent and beauty, so that it seemed that the red lips and the black eyeliner were overkill. Maggie wore a vintage, cherry-print dress. She'd cut a few inches off but her hair still fell into perfect ringlets, framing her heart shaped face. Yula had all but butchered her own hair in hopes of being taken more seriously, and Saul had changed nothing. He wore lots of brown. He let the girls talk and sing. That was more than enough.

Maggie didn't drive, so it was Yula who picked her up and drove her into the guts of Glory Town to Main Street, to where all things artsy and musical were designated, even limited to. On their drive they talked about Saul and music and college and how they both wanted everything to change, everything from their breasts to their hair to politics, to their college majors. Nothing was so bad it needed changing, but their youth demanded it, like a parasite in an all too acquiescing host.

During the show Maggie surveyed her audience, found a sea of familiar faces: former teachers, old high school and middle school flames, her mother's best friend, her brother's girlfriend, even her childhood dentist. While initially it felt warm and easy, to Maggie the coziness also felt deadening. Just before Maggie's voice lost a sliver of its magic, she caught site of a bright red tuft of hair at the back of the crowd. From a distance, and without her glasses, Maggie mistook Abby for a boy, a man that is. But as the bodies of so many familiars shifted and swayed, Abby's incongruous breasts came into full view. Maggie didn't know why, but she suddenly felt embarrassed about the jar that sat in front of Yula's keyboard stand: the jar with its garish announcement of their college-kid ways, their need for sweaty handfuls of cash for things like nail polish remover, donuts and Red bull.

When Maggie and Yula sang *Summertime*, Maggie saw the tall, lean body belonging to the red tuft of hair swaying. A smiled curled up in Maggie's belly. This song could last forever, she thought. But the song came to an end in one long, sweeping note. The crowd dissipated but that swaying body, waving its red flag, stood by.

Abby stood half dizzy and flushed after the last note of music played. It wasn't until a small boy bumped her leg with his doughy elbow that Abby spun around and realized that aside from passersby she could no longer count on a curtain of warm bodies to shield her excitement, her eagerness. In fact, for the first time in a year, Abby held Maggie in her direct gaze and Maggie with her little red mouth and her curious eyes held her own.

To begin with Abby offered a wave and an ugly smile. Abby kept her lips tight, not showing her teeth and pushed her bottom lip up against her top, like an old man caught without his dentures. But even so, Maggie waved and parted her lips. Does she remember me? Does she think it's strange? Does she think I'm strange?

But before any of Abby's insecurities were to be validated or dismissed a round and commanding woman stepped between herself and Maggie. It was Maggie's mother, Catherine. Beaming with pride, Catherine barely resisted grabbing her daughter's face by her powder dusted cheeks, and Abby, though never having been a mother herself, recognized the cost of holding back in the mother's expression.

When the mother turned around, Abby could feel Catherine taking her in. Though Abby had changed her appearance drastically, though Abby had clung to shadows for several years attempting to blend in and survive the waves of gossip that once crushed her, she detected in Catherine's gaze a puzzled recognition.

"Hello," Catherine offered, her eyebrows locked in a question.

"Hello," Abby returned, "Your daughter is so talented."

"Isn't she though?" Catherine finally unlocked her eyes from

Abby's disguise and returned a loving stare towards her daughter. Abby finally exhaled.

The mother like the jar was a sharp, unwelcome reminder of Maggie's gaudy dependence and lack of sophistication. If only she were worldly. She couldn't understand at the moment why it was that this lean, big-bosomy figure standing erect a few feet away triggered such a specific insecurity.

Yula was luckily at Maggie's rescue—quickly flocking to Catherine, offering up hugs and compliments. Saul cracked his knuckles and emptied the glass jar, counting the afternoon's bounty. As ejected as Maggie felt from her usual wealth of confidence and charisma, she still refused to cower. She returned her attention and her smile towards the Bowie-esque person before her. The tall person approached her finally, with her mother and her band-mates occupied, she finally reached out her hand to Maggie and said, "Hi, I'm Abby."

Abby had been married three times. Her first husband Elliot drowned while skinny-dipping with his secret lover. Abby never felt though that this was karma, or that he "got what he deserved." He was young, nineteen, and she was twenty. His belly and heart were full of mistakes waiting to be made. She thought always how tragic it was. To this day, she still exchanged Christmas cards and birthday cards with the girlfriend.

The second husband, Martin, reminded Abby a great deal of her father—cold, efficient, strong. He built a house with his huge, capable hands. Abby got pregnant twice, both times ending in miscarriage. After that, he wasn't so much cold, as he was desperate and sad. He built more rooms but each room swelled with emptiness. He could not go on. Abby could. Abby left and Martin found a woman who gave him whole children, fat and perfect babies with juicy, gruesome cries.

The last was Abraham. Abraham with his broad shoulders, his easy looks, Abraham with his empty bottles and overflowing cups, Abraham with his curly laugh and his long, thick penis. Abraham who turned heads, Abraham with the electric touch, the smile that you felt in your legs and kidneys and cunt. Abraham had stirred Abby up in ways other men hadn't.

Abby was in the car when it happened. People might never forgive her for letting him drive, but Abraham knew his smooth talk, what buttery words to use, "I'm all good, believe me, believe me, I know better. Good as gold." Believe me.

She had believed. Abby believed even when the reports said that the three-year-old twins were killed in the crash. She'd believed.

That's when Abby couldn't go on. Abraham and Abby were both hospitalized, the mother and father of the twins in comas. Abraham went to prison after he recovered from his injuries. In prison he found one Jesus and lost one Abby. Abby went on without her own permission. Abby carried the dead children from the car wreck in her swollen veins. The guilt rode her and sucked the color from her skin, her hair, and her eyes.

But even guilt dies, at least, old pages of guilt. Yet new pages write themselves every day. How to kill those too?

Yula said, "Tell me everything."

Three weeks had passed since Abby introduced herself to Maggie after the show. Three weeks of Maggie blushing. Three weeks of Maggie biting her lip and standing on tip toes and three weeks of Catherine asking and wondering and Maggie politely but not so innocently shrugging it away.

Maggie said, "I don't know. It's interesting. I don't know what to say."

At this point Saul pressed her, "Are you a thing? Like, an item? Does your mom know?"

How could Maggie tell them everything? She wasn't sure what the "everything" was. She knew this: It started quite honestly by accident. That is, bumping into Abby downtown. Literally. Meaning, their bodies made contact each time. Bump a shoulder. Graze an elbow. Bump, bump, bump. Maggie would say, "Abby, right?" And Abby would nod, say, "Hello Maggie. Nice to see you." And Maggie's throat would grow cold but moist and she'd feel something dancing in her ribs. The accidents continued, bump, bump, bump. Until finally Abby said, "I'd like to see you. On purpose. Sometime." And Maggie said, "How about now?" And that's when the accidents slid off the table and down the street and they walked to the park and ate strawberries on the bench, Maggie in her flirty skirt, Abby in her trousers and dark eyeliner, Abby staring off past the tree-line at the water and Maggie staring at Abby and Maggie touching Abby's knee with her bare knee and Abby looking down at her naked legs, then into her eyes and finally, a kiss, and hands on thighs and then and then, and she guessed that must be the "everything" but somehow it still wasn't and she couldn't bear to give Yula that and let Yula think, 'That's it?" She couldn't bear to give her "the everything" that really wasn't The Everything. So she said, "I just don't know." And Yula and Saul looked at one another and then at her and said, "Whatever."

Abby lived in an Airstream with an old dog named Atticus. To pay bills she prepared people's taxes. She made most her income during tax season and the rest of the year did bookkeeping from her home for a handful of small businesses. Her Airstream sat on a lot belonging to a local doctor in the woods, encircled by evergreens. This was Abby's home: a collection of ties, three from each husband, except Abraham who only owned one tie which he wore to their wedding, an ashtray turned paperweight, a book of poetry by e.e. cummings, The Little Prince, and a Bible. This was also Abby's home: Service for one, a flatulent, nine-year-old Irish Wolfhound, a dog bowl, a quilt of stars, a vibrator tucked under a red pillow. This too was Abby's home: A framed picture of John Wayne, autographed. A bottle of men's aftershave. A white dress worn three times. An urn holding her father's ashes. A small CD player. Maggie's homemade CD. Dylan. Bowie. Cash. The Beatles. More Dylan. Elvis. Hendrix. More Dylan.

But when Maggie came to visit, this was Abby's home: Porcelain curves. Slender giggles. Abby's fingers running through Abby's black curls, sighs light as air but succulent and wet. This too was Abby's home: Maggie whispering, "Promise you'll come see me when I go back to school. Promise you'll keep in touch." And this: "For as long as you want me to, I will."

And again, this was Abby's home: Maggie smoothing the sheets, leaving Abby's bed sharper than before, Maggie standing in pink bra and underwear as she fluffed the pillows and stacked them. Maggie singing while she dressed. Maggie in her perfect dress leaving to make her curfew. Maggie drowning in the evergreens as she waved goodbye, Goodbye for now. Goodbye.

This was Abby's house: Abby alone but for Atticus. Abby in her wife-beater and boxers. Abby reaching for the picture between the pages once more. Abby sobbing. Abby knowing. Abby hoping. Abby asking with her hand buried deep between her legs.

❧

On a Saturday night, Maggie played her last show of the summer with Yula and Saul and she could tell: They both wore sour news on their faces. Catherine had approached them earlier, they said. Catherine brought them cookies and smiles. Catherine wanted to know about the Everything that was Maggie and Abby. Yula and Saul told Catherine they knew nothing which was far from everything and Catherine had set down the plate filled with cookies and pulled out an article from her purse. It was an article about Abby printed off the internet, at least it was Abby's name they said, but it was a picture of a sad, weathered looking Abby and an story about dead children and a drunk driver. But Abby wasn't the driver, Yula chimed in, A man did it, Saul said. But that wasn't all, Yula said. Catherine told them that Abby had a dark, dark past: three marriages and the accident, and This. And that's when Catherine had pulled out another black and white page with a picture of a little boy. It was Abby but not Abby. That is, Yula started, Abby was a boy? But she said it like a question because in truth, Yula didn't know and really no one really did, and that is what she told Maggie.

But all Maggie could think about was Abby, her Abby with some bristly man. Her Abby with men. Men with clumsy penises. Men with thick necks. Men with hairy scrotum and bad breath. She did not care about accidents, or androgynous school pictures. She cared about what those bodies did with Abby's body which was now part of Maggie's body in stolen moments under a quilt and red pillow. She suddenly had the urge to pat her body in every place Abby had also touched her, as if to make sure it was all still there. But what she found was that more existed now than before. That Abby had breathed new parts into Maggie's young skin and now she was more than just Girl or Person and she felt so dizzy she began to cry. Yula and Saul each took one side of her body, trying to press comfort into her bones. But they didn't, they couldn't understand what parts needed healing and what parts just needed watering.

This was why Abby had let her hair grow shapeless and colorless for so many years. This was why Abby dressed like a Crone and waited for God to get down to business. This was the reason Abby lived in the woods with her friend dog. This was the reason Abby had an unlisted number. This was why Abby kept the ties close and picture closer. This was why Abby had lived like a snail. This was why: because of the Catherines, because of such bodies born with absolute sureness of gender, with no capacity to measure the pain in others less sure, and much less absolute.

Because of the Catherines.

But Maggie, she thought. Maggie she always thought. Maggie was worth it. Maggie who told Abby, "Boys have handled me like a Rubix cube. Not like you, like how you inhale me, and then when you breathe me out some parts of me are on fire and some parts are covered in goose bumps."

Yes, Abby felt the shell breaking. Yes, she knew that one Catherine could multiply into an army of Catherines and those Catherines could paint Abby's picture in blood and between her legs they would paint a sloppy dick and balls. They'd maybe paint horns on her head. They'd maybe draw a red, red circle around the misconstrued assumptions of her body and paint a bold slash over the whole mess of their composition of Abby, this stranger, this woman they did not, could not know.

But Maggie. Maggie and her soft legs. Maggie and her velvet songs. Maggie coursed through her veins, reinforced the unprotected layers, the swollen and vulnerable cracks of Abby's uniform. But were they enough to withstand the sharp edged swords of each and every Catherine in town?

Maggie had given this: Her virginity. Her songs. Her sex. Her lips. Her delicacy. Her brazenness. Her reputation. Her confidence. Abby returned what she could. Having almost twenty years on

Maggie, her gifts weren't the same. Abby had courage and that courage carried her sometimes half hazzardly towards Maggie, sometimes even right through her. Abby knew what she needed to give Maggie before the summer ended and it was a gift she was terrified to give. That's how Abby knew it was The One. It was her story and her story was this:

"My parents called me Archer, after my dad. They dressed me like a boy, they called me son and sometimes junior. Mom was a nurse. When I got sick it was mom that doctored me up. When I turned five and I was about to start school my parents started acting nervous. Dad bought me a fire engine the night before my first day. He told me how I could be a fireman or policeman or a president, man. 'But don't forget, you'll always be my boy,' he told me.

"I liked kindergarten. The kids were really nice and my teacher Mrs. Joyce was this sweet, tiny, pretty thing, a lot like you. She was a sweetheart. Everything was going great until the first bathroom break. I was still young enough that when I was out with my parents I'd use the ladies room with mom.

"When I pulled down my pants in front of the boys they knew I was different. They started saying, 'Hey, you're a girl! Archer's a girrrrl.'

"I got angry and yelled back and asked why they were saying that to me. This boy, I think he was named Paul, he said, 'Cause you don't have a wiener!' and another boy said, 'A penis! You don't have a penis.'

"When I got home as you can imagine, I was a complete mess and I told my parents what happened."

"What did they say? How did they try to explain it?" Maggie asked.

"They told me I was just a late bloomer, that lots of boys are late bloomers and that my penis just hadn't bloomed yet. I asked when it would happen and they just said, you'll see, it will happen. Be patient.'

"A year had passed and still no penis blooming. By then my parents had another baby and named her Shawn. The first time I saw them change her diaper I noticed she looked just like me. I asked how do they know she's not a boy, a late bloomer? But mother didn't answer, she just smiled and asked me to fetch her some baby lotion.

"That night I couldn't sleep. I heard Shawn cry and I went to her room. I had to see her, down there, I had to make sure she wasn't a boy with a late blooming penis, like me. I was only six…I didn't know.

"When my parents found me inspecting the baby's privates they hit me, then they hit me harder. They told me I was never allowed around the baby again. They called me a pervert.

"They kept me home from school for several days and then Mrs. Joyce, who thought I should do another year with her—got worried. She made a home visit and when she saw the shape I was in, well, you can imagine…I never saw them again."

"Good Good riddance!" Maggie said, face growing flushed, "I bet you were relieved."

"No, not at all. They did terrible things, but they were all I knew of family. I was petrified. Not only that but when the doctor examined me thinking I was a-six year-old boy named Archer, he just about had a heart attack and his shock just about gave me one too. An endless parade of therapists and social workers came through. A heavy set older woman with a high-pitched voice came in and started asking questions. She brought books and asked what I knew about the birds and the bees. I shrugged and said bees buzz and birds sing, both can fly and both start with the letter "B". She said I was a very smart little girl. Something about the way she said it made me cry.

"She opened the books and showed me lots of embarrassing pictures. I saw myself in some of them. She said, 'Girls have vaginas and boys have penises.' I told her that my penis just hadn't grown yet, and that I was a late bloomer.

"She said nothing back. In fact she left the room and didn't come back, even though she said she was going to. Instead a man in a suit came in. He was all serious and hollow."

Because Maggie was young and beautiful she was also impatient. She understood why she needed to hear all about Archer and the awful parents. But Maggie wanted, needed, to know about the husbands. She wanted to know why Abby married them and why she left them. She like so many young lovers in their first serious love affair, Maggie wanted to catalog the truancies and misdemeanors so she could avoid them, so she could be the last love of all. Maggie asked:

Did you love them?

What did you love about them?

Why did you stop loving them?

How much did you love them?

Do you miss them?

Do you love me as much as you loved them?

What if your love for me runs out?

How can you be sure?

Will you tell me?

Do you promise?

How do I know you mean it?

A quieter voice inside told Maggie to stop and listen. That same voice whispered, 'Not now, not now, shh and make love, shhh and bury your head in her lap, don't do this, please...' But that voice was too quiet and too docile to teach a girl in love anything.

Abby had only one answer for all of Maggie's questions. She pulled Maggie onto her back, spread her legs apart, kissed her breasts, looked into her eyes, and thrust. Maggie gave a surprised little gasp.

Abby said, "My parents were right about me. I was, I am, a late bloomer."

When Yula and Saul drove Maggie to the airport they didn't ask questions. Maggie knew why. For the first time in their unapologetically young lives their trio had encountered The Sacred. The thing that becomes so much The Everything that it is no longer something you can divulge on a drive to the airport or on a drive to anywhere for that matter. It wasn't the same as a secret, its roots were deeper, older. As Maggie felt the memories of Abby and the summer trickle down her throat, she also traced them on her neck as if to make sure they'd always be a part of her.

When the silence overstayed its welcome Yula began to sing We Built this City and Saul laughed and poked Yula's shoulder and Maggie could tell they'd had sex again. Saul sang too, and Maggie joined in eventually as she finally remembered what life was like before.

Atticus licked the tears off Abby's cheeks until she pushed him away, drying off both tears and saliva with her red pillow.

Abby added a second picture between the pages of her Little Prince book: a picture of Maggie singing, her eyes closed, her bright, white hands cradling the microphone, the summer sky framing her in the sharpest shade of blue. No one else in the photo. In the sky. In the world. No Catherines. No Abbys either. Just the girl who finally made her a man.

The Need

She wasn't madly in love anymore, she was just mad. She wondered what would happen if she stopped acting like a wife to her husband. That is if she quit offering up the pleasing, wifely things that he'd grown accustomed to. If she stopped asking him how his day was, if she stopped picking up his dirty socks, if she stopped offering up her crotch like a dinner roll.

Her husband had bought her an aquarium on their first wedding anniversary on account of her love of fish and the sea. Because of the fish she was able to hold onto her love for him a little while more. But three years had passed. She still loved the fish but she tolerated her husband.

She wasn't sure why it was that it would always wear off. She'd fall in love like a trapeze artist and within weeks or months an unseen force stole away the passion right from under her skin and no Amber Alert could ever bring it back. The touch that once excited her and set her blood on fire now turned her guts into reckless and heavy knots. She could barely keep her coffee down when he climbed on top of her.

She thought about quitting being a wife every day until the thoughts consumed her completely. Occasionally her husband would ask if something was the matter, but she shut him up with one type of dinner roll or another. When her husband left for the day, she sat in front of her aquarium and told the fish her troubles. Garish fish eyes stunned by her attention glared back. Sometimes she dipped her fingertips in the water and some of the braver fish nibbled at her flesh. She liked it so much she started dipping her whole hand in the water. She kept her hand and her fingers very still and when a bolder fish swam close enough she'd try to close her fingers around his wiggly body. Then she'd let go. She did this several times a day, to the point of forgetting sometimes how mad she was. Water had this effect on her.

One day her husband came home and found her kneeling on a stool she'd set up next to the aquarium. She had leaned as far as she could into the aquarium until her head was submerged.

Her husband dropped his briefcase and lunchbox and screamed, "Whatthehellareyoudoing!?"

She couldn't hear him with her face plunged into the murky water. But she could see his face reddening, his fists clenched. Before he could touch her she raised her head out the water and didn't say a word. She dragged the stool away from the aquarium and placed it back at the bar in the kitchen where it belonged.

That night, he climbed on top of her again wanting her to look at him, but she could not.

"Let's fill the tub," she suggested. She filled the tub and climbed inside. But when he plunged his massive feet into the tub, water flowed over the sides and flooded the bathroom. She started to get up but he said, No, no, Don't worry about that now. But she did worry. His entrance was graceless and clumsy. Not like a fish. There was no tender nibbling. Instead he approached her like a tsunami and his passion just about drowned her.

When she came up for air her husband was already stepping out of the tub. He walked thick and sopping across the flooded floor and collapsed onto their bed, falling fast asleep. The water had turned cold and she began to cry and shake. Some of her husband's pubic hairs rose to the surface and she cried even harder. Still naked and trembling, she drained the water until the tub was empty and shuffled her way to the kitchen to retrieve a pitcher. She used the pitcher to gather up fish and aquarium water to refill the tub. She could not risk shocking the fish to death with the temperature of the bathwater. She made several trips back and forth from the aquarium to the bathtub until the aquarium was completely empty of both fish and water. By the last trip she was no longer wet, and her goose bumps had faded. Ever so slowly, she descended into the tub where her fish swam freely in their own waste-ridden water.

She laid back and spread her legs apart, resting one foot on either corner of the tub. The smell of the water reminded her of the beach at low tide and of her first period. It was putrid and sweet. Her fish company scattered in different directions. The tetras tickled the inside of her floating arms, while the goldfish blew bubbles in her tangled hair. The cichlids swam between her legs, dug gently into her fleshy cave. She fell asleep to a wave of spasms in her womb that left her face flushed and warm.

In the morning her husband found her in the tub with all the fish and it turned his stomach so much to see the filth in the water clinging to his wife's breasts and face and hair that he vomited and the retching woke her up. Before he could say a word she told him, "We need a bigger aquarium."

To her surprise he said, "Yes, sure, I'll buy you the biggest aquarium I can find, just don't ever do that again."

"I won't empty the aquarium in here ever again if you find me a much bigger aquarium. I promise."

"Okay," he nodded, "I'll get you what you need."

She rose from the water feeling changed, not in the way of a new convert, but in the way that one does after one knows death for the first time. The way in which one nods at a funeral and says, "Yes, I've lost a loved one too, quite recently." She was now one of those people who knew about death, who could talk about it if she had to, could comfort devastated widows if she wanted to. Some pieces of waste slipped off of her, but the algae clung on. Two goldfish were tangled in her hair as she climbed out and one hit the bathroom floor and started his flipping and flopping. Casually she reached down and returned him to the water before reaching into her cold matted hair to retrieve his partner.

"You must be freezing!" her husband said touching her cheek. But she was very warm.

Standing naked before him, her flat nipples like little pink buttons, she asked, "Do you promise you will get me that big aquarium? I mean huge. Huge."

He nodded and reached for her breasts, surprised at the heat of their temperature. Water dripped from her vagina and a small cichlid slid down her leg. Her husband didn't notice.

When he left for work she didn't bother to clean the vomit in or around the toilet.

What she did was refill the aquarium. What she did was carry each fish comrade safely back home. What she did was shower and to scour her deadened skin as if to find another layer. What she did was close her eyes and imagine scrubbing off her skin and finding fish scales instead. What she did was smile and touch herself as she thought of the fish and water between her legs and dripping off her breasts. What she did was cry when she opened her eyes and found she'd rubbed her still human layer red and raw.

What she didn't do was make dinner. What she didn't do was put on make-up and panty hose. What she didn't do was make the bed or wash the dishes. What she didn't do was eat or drink or talk for the day. What she knew was this: she was dead inside of a live body.

When her husband came home that night he said, "I have something for you—"

And she felt some of that horny blood fire for him, until he opened the door wider and revealed a boyish girl in cords with wide shoulders and short blond hair and he said, "You have help now." And he sent the boyish girl make the bed and to make the dinner and to wash the sheets and even to feed the fish which was the last straw.

"That's not an aquarium," was all she could say.

He promised her soon the aquarium would come, that he had to special order it.

"That way, and until then," he told his wife, "Everything still gets done like before."

Chore by chore, the boyish girl had erased the need-to-be-done-things from their home.

So she did what she had to do. While the boyish girl busied herself scrubbing caked vomit off the bathroom tile, the wife emptied the aquarium into her tub and lay back inside with all the fish. The water was much clearer, cleaner. Honestly, it wasn't the same without that smell.

The boyish girl said, "You must really love fish," and the boyish girl raised her eyebrows, and the boyish girl was definitely not wearing a bra though the boyish girl had not much breasts anyway which is why she was a boyish girl to begin with. And the boyish girl kept smiling even as the scent of dried vomit and fishy water filled the room, even as her question went unanswered, the boyish girl smiled with her mouth, her cheeks, her eyes, she even smiled with her legs. The smile filled up the bathroom and even the fish and the warm-blooded woman among them felt the wake of the boyish girl's smile in their exclusive water.

"I wanted an aquarium. A giant aquarium. Not a person. There are already so many people."

She finally answered the boyish girl this way, and the boyish girl beamed even brighter.

"I like that," the boyish girl said.

Just then the husband reappeared having just finished the dinner cooked by the boyish girl, with a bit of gin on his breath, loosening his tie, while his pants tightened over the full, hard member between his legs. He asked the boyish girl to leave the bathroom, to clean the kitchen and the table, to clean the counters and wash the dishes and to make his lunch for tomorrow and the boyish girl's smile locked on her face into something rigid and unsettling.

"You promised," the husband said.

"So did you," said his wife, and she closed her eyes but the tears came all the same.

That night, the wife dreamed a cruel kind of dream, because it gave her what she wanted and what she did not have. She dreamed that when she woke she was a lady fish, not something as obvious as a mermaid mind you, but a lady fish. She still had all her same body parts, her chubby vagina, her little apple breasts. But she was covered in iridescent scales. The house itself was her aquarium and she could know the fish's thoughts and they could know hers, sometimes her husband knocked on the glass of their aquarium home to get her attention, but mostly he didn't. And the spaces between her and the fish took on the shape and movement of the boyish girl's smile and the smile carried them and exhausted them all at once. The smile lived sometimes inside those shapes between them, and sometimes inside them where the breathing happened. All in all, it was a beautifully wicked vision and when she woke she wondered how the dead could still dream.

The Guppy Suicides

Maggie was still in pigtails and pampers when her guppies leapt out of the fishbowl. On the carpet they looked nothing like fish but more like specks of fabric. She squished them with her naked heel then confessed to her mother who told her that such little things are temporary anyway.

She was only two years older when she asked her father to kill the mouse she'd found in her toy box. She had tried herself. To step on it would have made a mess so Maggie tried Saran Wrap, but the mouse kept breathing. She dropped the scurrying mouse in a jar and handed it to her father. Maggie watched to see how he would deal with it. He broke a branch off the apple tree and stabbed the mouse until the glass went red then he tossed the jar into dumpster and threw the branch to the curb.

Maggie was nine when she noticed the bird didn't fly away no matter how close she got. She bent over to pick it up and it opened its beak. Maggie dipped her finger in the bird bath and let a drop fall into the bird's mouth. Her mother said, "Don't touch that, it's dirty." So Maggie hid the bird inside of her dress and snuck her into her bedroom.

The bird would not eat or drink. Its chest rose and fell. Maggie waited. No song came. No chirping, only the struggle to breathe.

When the bird died in Maggie's trembling palms, she took a ceramic bowl from her mother's cabinet and a roll of paper towels. She wrapped the dead bird in some towels and placed it in the center of the bowl. Maggie buried the bird inside its casket bowl in the very back corner of the yard, beyond the strawberries and lettuce. She drove a stake into the loose dirt to mark the grave.

A week later, Maggie wondered if she'd been wrong about the bird. The dirt was still loose enough she could dig with her hands. She felt the bowl and lifted it out of the hole. The small mass inside the paper towel was still soft. She unraveled the paper towel. Yellow goo fused the bird to the paper. Maggie held her breath, wrapped the bird up again, stuck it in the bowl, and pushed the dirt back on top. She threw the stake over the fence.

Some goo and a small feather stuck to the end of Maggie's forefinger. She couldn't shake it off. She passed some daisies, knelt down, and rubbed the petals to peel the feather off. A bee buzzed near her arm, and Maggie felt the sting. The red mark on her arm began to swell. But Maggie told no one.

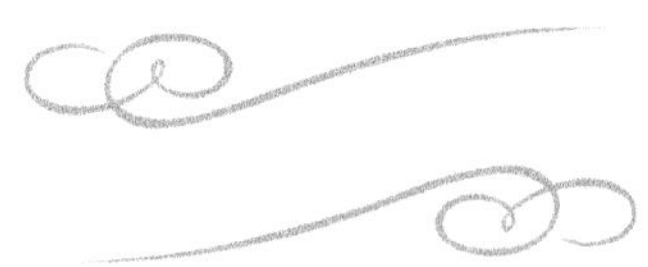

The Conscience of Spiders

(In memory of outsider artist Henry Darger.
April 12, 1892 to April 13, 1973)

Before I was a woman, I was a spider. My footsteps were silent. Cold, dark places were my home. I took what I needed and left the excess. No one told me what I was. I was born knowing it all, my purpose, my strength, and my prey.

Eventually I tired of the basement's dank, moldy laundry. I wanted to nest in a higher place, to know the world at a distance, guarding my solitude with anonymity. That is how I came upon the old janitor.

He was called Henry Darger. I spun a web inside his apartment window. Other curious spiders joined me and Henry's quiet audience grew. His apartment never knew day from night, and no one knew him but us.

We watched him glue portraits of baby-faced girls to watercolor landscapes stretched across the walls, the floor. Henry painted his heroes the Vivian Girls—little girls with penises who fought off monsters and men in military coats. We his spider daughters argued amongst ourselves. Is he a deviant or an innocent? Some decided he was the pornographer gone mad in his isolation. Others like me decided he was a child, clueless of the rules. The only undecided Daughter of Darger silently crawled across a wet painting until she reached the face of an unfinished pig-tailed girl, and blossomed from the child's mouth like a tiger lily.

Henry's thick, coarse, and charcoal stained hands are unspoken evidence of invented magic, places lit by his imagination. That's when I envied the dreaming. Henry, in your dreams do the little girls defeat the evil monsters in the Glandolinian War? In your dreams have you spotted me, your protector of secrets?

Henry's life took place on pages, tens of thousands of pages. But sometimes words were spoken into the deceivingly empty apartment. One year Henry cursed God for the snow, cursed the church for leaving him both fatherless and childless. These are moments I was tempted to reveal myself, but I knew Henry was a maker, something more than an ordinary man, capable of creating his desired company. I was superfluous.

In Henry's room, there were no empty bottles of liquor or wine, no excess articles of clothing strewn about the room. And in the thousands of pictures piled, stacked and sometimes scattered, there were no traces of Henry's past, only the traced, drawn and painted faces of his little girl heroines, the pillars of his blooming story.

Henry is a snowflake in hell. My capsule of a body carries the hot poison that could melt him. But I want him to finish and I want the little girls to steal the waves of grass back from the dragons and soldiers. I want to know that the littlest beings can show the Giants the secret places they've been missing.

Thousands of water colored pages later, our Henry dies in his sleep. Not on his mattress which was buried in pages, but in his chair, at his desk, still in navy-blue janitor overalls, his hands and head resting on his latest collage of the Vivian Girls, who'd claimed the final victory.

People enter his sanctuary, our sanctuary. Strangers interpret the old janitor's room. A woman in a pompous yellow hat calls him a recluse. The word rings true, resonates with me. I am the same. I spring towards the yellow to become a star atop the woman's hat. I am invisible, her worst fear.

Little did I know that once I released my venom into the woman's skin, I'd be caught and killed and this would be my last life as a spider, a small, unnoticed predator. If I had known that I would be reborn as the very same thing I poisoned, would I have let the strangers interpret our Henry's works without interference?

In my new body I am a clumsy mess. Now gaudily visible I can no longer disappear into cracks, or make homes of windowsills and curtains. Even houses won't conceal me.

Though I'm a woman now, I sometimes remember having been very small, and having hung from high places. In my home the smallest, most hidden places take precedence and I welcome silent visitors. The venom of my new existence is Time. I wait for the next rebirth. I ache for a transformation to be once again a selective danger.

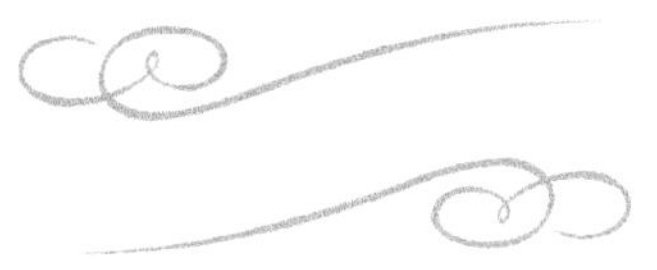

A Letter to My Friend Who is Dying

Iknow a lot more than you think I do, for instance, I know that you are going to die very soon. I've known since early March, the day you had your ladies over for poker, remember? I do because that night I ate salmon and you know how salmon is my favorite. I smelled something each time I walked close to you, every time you touched me. I struck you out of fear, because you didn't smell like you. You had the scent of a wandering stranger, far from home, far from health. The thin skin on your wrist where I scratched you tore a little. You bled, and when you bled, I knew without a doubt. Your blood has been screaming with it ever since.

When you die, I'll be sent to live with your sister Mona, or as I call her MOAN-a. I'll have to put up with her horrible little dogs; the ones that she lets lick her face for an awkward length of time. Under her guardianship, I'll end up hiding in the spare room all day, missing the garden. In the garden I feel like the world belongs to just us. You sit in your cedar bench, with your yellow sunhat and your books. I still sit by your side every afternoon, even now that you smell like a dead mole, like dog's breath, like the kitchen when the food is left out overnight. You're tired, more than usual, but you haven't caught on yet. No one has but me.

That time I spent a week at Mona's home--I still haven't forgiven you for that just so you know-- she was watching one of her favorite programs. It was hosted by a man who could read minds and tell people things they didn't know. He'd pick random audience members and tell them their dead dad or aunt or mother or father said to move on, where they left the secret stash of money, or how they really died. Mona sat on the couch with her ghastly little dogs, her pug, her yorky, and worst, her bug eyed Chihuahua donning a pink tutu and matching collar. Mona cried when the people on TV cried and she took down the number at the end of the show because I guess she wants that strange man to tell her things she doesn't know.

Why would anyone want to know about something they can do nothing about? I know that you will die, and I know that your death will be painful. I can smell the pain. I didn't need a strange man with orange skin to tell me. When you know someone, the way I know you, the truth of things will find a forgotten place inside you to crawl inside of and to whisper, "This is how it will be, this is what will happen." Mona wants to know something she doesn't. I would un-know what I know if I could.

When you die, no one else in the world will see what you see in me, what you've always seen. How long have I lived with you, seventeen years? Since I was a tiny little thing. Remember how terrified I was? I hid under the covers. I hid in corners and dark cabinets. When you are gone, I will be that terrified again, maybe even more. So I've decided what will happen to me when you die: I will join you.

I'm not sure how to do it yet. I don't want to die a gruesome death, but I don't want to die like a coward either. Don't think I'm romanticizing the taking of my own life, or your untimely death. I'm being pragmatic. You see, I've had a lovely time with you, quite lovely, lovelier than I ever imagined. Why live out the rest of my years without you, you who made my world so lovely?

I know you've been worried for me, thinking I'm the one with only a little time left, afraid that I will leave you. Don't worry my friend. I'll be here right until the end. Nurses and fair-weather friends, Mona and her bulimic dogs, they will come and go. Not me. I will be here until the last breath and then I will follow you into the ominous Next Place.

When you die there will be no one left for me, not really. Someone—maybe Mona, maybe not-- may feed me, give me shelter, and occasionally attempt to show me affection in spite of my hostility. But no one will ever look at me again and think, "There's my friend, my very best friend." Once you're gone they will say, "There goes that old black cat, that stuck up cat with the long, gray whiskers," they will say, "How old is he anyway? Probably doesn't have much time left." I know I have more time than they would ever guess. At least, I would if I had you to grow old with. But I won't because the disease is taking over you, and it will continue eating you up until there's more disease than you.

For as aloof and independent as you believe me to be, I am quite fond of you. That is why I will follow you, purring, weaving between your legs, and I will never leave your side. Everyone should have that someone who never, ever leaves their side, no matter what. I will go with you, because you are the lady who calls me Friend, when the rest of the world calls me Cat.

Wolf Story

Maria had a dream about a fat boy who led a parade of blind people and spry deer. She knew the boy at least, was real. Monday afternoon she'd seen him pedal his red bike past a caution sign and bright orange traffic cones. He rode with a pink frosted donut half hanging from his mouth.

The next morning on her drive to work she stopped her car for a skinny wolf trying to cross the street. Previous cars weren't so thoughtful and the young wolf had been waiting all morning, growing hungrier for the stillness only she gave him. The wolf lurked as far as the start of the pavement, beyond the edge of the woods. He sat and smiled towards Maria.

Maria took this as an invitation and started to call him.

"Here boy," she guessed, "Come here."

Without even bothering to check the time, or concern herself with getting to the office, Maria opened her car door and whistled for the wolf to come inside.

Being young and without the necessary doubts that age and wisdom bring, the young wolf's hunger lulled him inside. He climbed onto the passenger seat, panting happily.

Inside her apartment, Maria dropped her keys into a bowl and removed her shoes without using her hands, only the heels and toes of her feet. She patted her thigh and gave a sharp, short whistle to let the wolf know, he was safe. The wolf abandoned all timidity at the scent of burnt toast and coffee. He trotted quickly into Maria's kitchen and stood on his hind legs, his paws on the counter, sniffing the toaster.

"You must be starved!" Maria said, "Maybe I interrupted your hunt. Whatever is mine is yours."

She offered a bran muffin. He politely declined, pushing it away with his black nose.

"Of course, not," she put her finger to her frowning lips.

Maria carefully considered the contents of her fridge, eggs, sausage, beans, yogurt, and apple cider. She offered a buffet style meal spread out the kitchen tile floor. But although she could hear the grumbling in the wolf's belly, he showed no interest in any of it.

Maria remembered something she read long ago, that to make peace with a wild thing you must offer them a gift, a living gift. And what other living thing did she have to offer but herself? It wouldn't be the first time, she thought, and so like she had so many other times in her life, she undressed. She stripped down to a pink bra and underwear. She laid herself out on the kitchen floor and closed her eyes.

The wolf tilted his head side to side, trying to make sense of her offering. Finally, he crawled over to her, hesitantly but with purpose.

He started with her toes, sniffing and licking, then her knees and the curve of her hip. He stopped at her navel and put his hear to her belly to listen, as though that's where her heart lived.

"Do you love me to the moon?" she asked, her eyes still closed.

But the wolf backed away from her.

"Do you love me to the sky?"

The wolf groaned and shook his head.

"Do you love me to the ceiling?"

Finally, the young wolf crept from her belly to her face, running his nose along her forehead.

"To the ceiling then? To the ceiling is pretty good."

In that moment of satisfaction, Maria's naked skin became like the earth beneath the forest, emitting the scent of every kind of prey, from fatty to dense, from those with wings, to those with hooves. Maria's body had become each and every one inside that answer.

The wolf started with her hair, which smelled like sick deer and wet leaves. He ate every strand and he was filled up.

Maria kept her eyes shut, her cool and unencumbered scalp new and sweet. She stroked the skin below her bellybutton.

"Right here," she said. "Put your head here."

Maria took both her palms, put them behind his ears, and massaged them with her thumb and forefinger. The wolf hummed a low hum, one like the static off the T.V., the vibration of the refrigerator.

But shortly after his "meal", the wolf began to moan. It was clear he was aching, maybe even dying. Maria sat up in a hurry, and put her hand to his arched back. She watched him heave and heave until he vomited a cocoon made of her hair.

"Poor thing, what have I done!"

She curled her naked torso closer to his weak body; with one hand still on his back she laid her other hand on his belly. The dry heaves continued, followed by a bowel-anchored howl. Maria watched as the wolf's throat engorged until finally he coughed up the culprit—a pair of red handlebars. The spent wolf trembled and fell to the floor.

"The boy?" Maria asked, "The boy on the red bike?"

But the wolf didn't answer. He only moaned.

"You ate the boy! You killed the boy on my bike! The boy from my dream!"

Maria yelled, pulling away from him.

But the wolf, looking even slighter than before, tried to crawl to her his front paws scooting towards her naked lap.

"This always happens to me! Why me?"

With that she grabbed her clothes and cursed the wolf a few more times.

Maria wrapped herself in her hair cocoon concealing her contours and curves. She left the wolf the apartment, keys, and car.

Barefoot she seemed to float into the nearby woods. Half a mile from her home Maria found the place where houses and streets vanish and only trunks and leaves remain. The sky's pale-blue fabric, an expanding roof ready to cave.

Meanwhile on a hidden street beyond the edge of the woods, a fat-faced boy parades his shiny new yellow bike, sterling compensation for his scraped knees, his slight bruises.

The Harvest

At age fifty, after three decades of rejection, Eldon marries an onion. Before the onion, Eldon had fallen in love with hundreds of women. They were always young, slender, and charming. The first woman he ever proposed to was named Lita, she had red hair and wore a pointy bra under pink angora. He said to her, "Lita, I love you. I want to marry you." To which Lita responded, "That's nice." He was twenty then. His sisters told him it was because he kept going for young and beautiful, and young and beautiful only want rich and richer.

Eldon picks apples and pears and sometimes cherries. He takes home the bruised apples and pears that cannot be sold. He saves boxes of them for winter. He carves apples into little half-moon shavings for dessert. Eldon believes that one day, a beautiful woman will love him because he's a hardworking, honest man. He believes this woman will listen to A.M. radio in the evenings with him, eat apples with him, and that life will be simple and good.

Eldon begins wearing hats because he thinks it will make him look sophisticated, distinguished and that women will like it. It works at first. When his face is shaven and his clothes are clean, Eldon doesn't look so bad, and with a hat putting on just the right amount of shadow over his eyes, well, he's damn attractive. At least, this is what Kathy and her friend Vivian think, as they watch him walk through the park, picking cherries from a paper bag, and popping them in his mouth. The two girls ask Eldon to drive them to places. Once, even to Montana to visit Vivian's diabetic aunt. But when Eldon tries to kiss Vivian-he put his hand to her face right before-Vivian steps back, she asks to be taken home.

These scenarios continue into Eldon's thirties, and forties. Apples turn into applesauce. Eldon's hats begin to slump like sad little mushrooms. Finally he leaves apple orchards for the onion fields. He desires something less sweet. When the onions stop growing they lose their color, weaken at the top of the bulb and flop over. Less experienced gardeners ask, "What's wrong?" Not Eldon. He knows this is Nature's plan. The leaves have put the last of their energy into the bulbs. Eldon also knows that there is no wrong time to pull an onion, as onions always have something to offer.

Eldon brings home the surplus. When he chops onions into cubes for soup he doesn't fall for the sting. His eyes do not well up with tears. But as he pulls the last onion, removes her brown, papery skin, he reveals a luminous, pearly white face. Her eyes search her new surroundings. Eldon runs his finger down the side of her face. She doesn't complain about the coarseness of his hands. Take me, her eyes say.

Eldon does just that. He says his vows and takes her to bed. He points out the window at the night sky and tells her the stars are hers. He kisses her tiny mouth. They fall to sleep in purrs.

Eldon is sixty. He keeps his wife inside his hat. In the evenings, he puts her in his lap. For dinner, always soup and tea. But this night stirs with the unexpected and Eldon sets his wife on the counter and answers the door. A woman in rags stands before him, her head bowed, her feet bare.

"Can I help you?" Eldon asks.

She lifts her eyes, just barely, and says, "I was young then. I didn't know."

Eldon recognizes Vivian beneath the sun-damaged skin, the faded gray color of her eyes.

Vivian presses Eldon's hand to her cheek. "Take me," she says.

Meanwhile, Eldon's onion-wife rolls off the counter, splitting into perfect, half-moons.

Crown

I held you in my arms after washing my hands in hot water and ivory soap for sixty seconds. That was the rule. At age eight, I believed myself an expert on how to hold new things, an expert of how to live in this noisy world. I smelled the top of your head, examined your frail fingernails. I gently flexed them, alarmed at how pliable they were. I tested mine: stiff, inflexible...already. I marveled at your softness, your absolute perfection.

When I was thirteen, I was more of an expert, and your parents asked, Can you keep your eyes on him please? And I did. You pouted, you stomped your foot while your parents busied themselves cleaning out their most recent rental, the third in one year. When I tried to take your hand in mine, an offering of comfort, you bit me. But I didn't tell. I understood it was your protest, the last straw of your patience as you watched your toys sorted, divided into labeled boxes, your clothes folded and lowered into ballooning duffel bags and plastic bins. I added the bite to my crown, a gem of my growing expertise on how to be.

When I was twenty, my crown heavy with dull rocks and broken stones, I watched you, together with my two-year-old son. You were playing with your train set, a birthday gift from your grandmother. My son stomped on the train, pulled pieces from the track, broke them in two, in three, even four, after ruthlessly chewing them up. You sat on the floor, looking at the wake of destruction my angry toddler left behind. I waited for your rage, the five-year-old who stomped his feet, who showed his teeth. But you didn't. Instead, you lifted your head, your glossy eyes questioning mine. I asked, Can it be fixed? You shook your head. No, you answered, But everything breaks, eventually.

You said, You just have to let it go once it's broken. Everything breaks, I repeated.

I was twenty-eight the next time we met and you were a man, towering over the shattered pieces of my crown. I was no expert on how to live. I had only taken too long to believe it. How many years has it been? I asked, knowing full well eight years had passed. Too many, you answered. My son still talks about you, I said. You hugged me, pressing the back of my head towards you, pulling my face into your chest. I drowned in your scent. I thought, This is what I've been waiting for. This. Nothing else.

It wasn't perfect the first time, or the second. Our first kiss flooded as November poured through a canopy of evergreens. You wiped my face with the inside of your coat, as if you'd forgotten it hadn't stopped raining. My face wouldn't stay dry and not only because of the rain.

You left. To find yourself, you said, to know yourself. You were just a kid who thought he was a man, you told me. You were still growing. You were only twenty when you talked about forever. You were no expert on how to be. Be angry, tell me how horrible I am for doing this to you, you begged. I rubbed the place on my left hand, the meaty part of my thumb where you'd taken a bite out of me so long ago. I told you, Everything breaks, eventually. You left me while I sat in the tub, my skin going up in flames. I wanted the scalding water to burn the flesh right off my bones, to rid me of tissue, of nerves, anything capable of drinking and retaining this pain. White bones, a ladder of broken steps to a broken heart.

I swear it's not too late. A place must exist where broken things are made whole again, where time exists windowless, insulating this tiny kingdom. I swear it's not too late, to cure the brokenness, to heal such subtle but profound damage. I swear it isn't too late to find yourself inside this room, with me. It's not too late, I say to you, when you come back to gather your things; a guitar, a presumably lost jersey, your bags of shirts stuffed inside Safeway bags. I tell you, I kept the pieces all these years, promised myself I'd fix the track, that I'd replace the joints between the train cars. I said, I know it's a long time coming, but broken things can be fixed.

But you left.

Night after night without you, the ages between us fight their bloody wars. I have loved you in every way, maybe even with a new love that never existed before me and you. Tell me it's not too late to put down our swords. Tell me it's not too late and I will believe you. I will sink into that ruthless dream. I will wait.

But you left.

I told you I would put this pain on paper. I told you I would bear it. This is me, my love, bearing it.

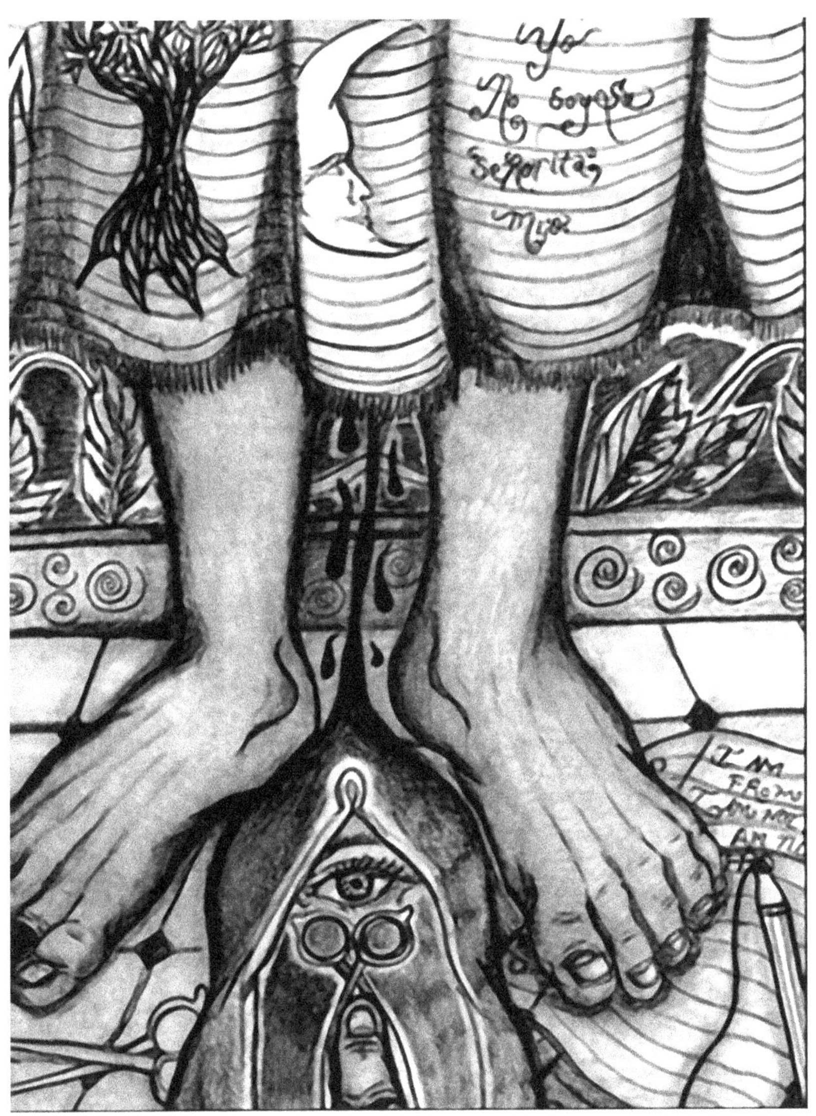
Yo
No soy su
Señorita,
Mijo
I'M
FROM
TOLUMNE
AN TO

Coco

Chapter 1
The Funeral

Too bad for Maribel, God gave her an extra arm, and too bad that her beautiful, olive-skinned mother went into such shock at the sight of her that her heart shattered and she died. Not that the arm itself was malformed or grotesque, but the fact that the arm protruded from the left side of Maribel's upper back and trembled with afterbirth proved more than Carmen's heart could take.

Daniel wrapped his wife in their wedding quilt, after his mother Elena had gently sponged clean Carmen's cold skin and dressed her in her *quinceañera* dress. Meanwhile, a slight, quiet Maribel slept nestled in a warm nest of fleece blankets Abuela Elena had prepared for her, inside a wicker basket at the foot of the bed.

Daniel and Elena saved their tears, deep inside their pockets. The ceremony, taking place only twenty-four hours after Carmen's death—for neither Daniel nor Elena could bear to let death's ugliness ravage their darling girl—was their greatest priority. The grief, the insurmountable loss of Carmen, as well as the ungodly, terrifying sight of Maribel's dysfunction, would have to wait.

Carmen's funeral took place in the back yard, near a bed of daisies. It had been the place where, on bended knee, Daniel had proposed to her. At the time, he had no ring to offer her. Instead he picked one of the daisies and tied it around her ring finger. This seemed to delight Carmen more than silver, or gold, or any gem ever would.

Though Carmen's parents had passed away years earlier, Carmen did not want for love. She was the gold-hearted beauty of the community, and it was her kindness that had stamped invisible tattoos upon every person who had ever become acquainted with her. Neighbors and friends of neighbors, and relatives of those friends and neighbors, attended Carmen's funeral, and somehow the Trozcos' little yard stretched to accommodate all of them. The heavy-hearted guests let their tears loose while Daniel and Elena nearly suffocated in their grief.

Only one guest arrived unwanted: Beatriz Fabo, who arrived carrying her healthy, two-armed and devastatingly beautiful baby boy. Beatriz had given birth to her son, Sammy, not only on the same day, but the same hour and same minute as Maribel also entered the world. That is when Elena believed without a doubt that Beatriz had given her beloved Carmen, *mal de ojo*, the Evil Eye.

Elena had desperately tried to warn Carmen during her pregnancy that she was much too beautiful. It was true: Carmen's beauty was both admired and coveted. But Elena was sure that Beatriz desired Carmen's beauty to the extent of committing great malice. For Beatriz Fabo was truly the homeliest woman Elena and the entire neighborhood, and maybe even the whole world, had ever laid eyes on.

Some women are tall and slender, others are petite and charming, some are round and glowing, some women slice the air with their sharp angles. But what could be said about poor Beatriz Fabo? She was a shadow of a shape in motion. Her face had the right parts but a jarring effect on onlookers. Her close-spaced, hooded eyes suggested a color, but never decided on one;

her skin was sallow down to her very lips, and her nose was a long, wavy line with no decipherable end. As an adult, Beatriz kept her thin brown hair cropped at chin length. In her youth, she had worn it very long while her mother and aunts decorated her locks with silk flowers and rhinestone-studded hair clips. They pulled and braided and brushed her hair into exquisite braids, into hairdos fit for a princess. They subjected her to permanent waves that smelled of sulfur and made her eyes sting. They bleached the dull brown from her hair, coloring it with dynamic reds, rich blue-blacks, or golden highlights. But what happens when you take a dilapidated house, rotting from the foundation up and only give it a coat of paint? Eventually, the damage on the inside comes through the façade. No amount of painting and primping can cure the state of wooden beams infested with termites; paint and new hardware cannot undo years of neglect, years of denial and superficial solutions. Beatriz was such a house. No amount of rouge and eyeliner, no amount of curling, twisting and scouring reached her foundation, the very core of her where no one had thought to look.

When Elena looked upon baby Sammy, her suspicions dug deeper into the earth and grew branches of validation. Beatriz had stolen Carmen's beauty, and Beatriz's greedy witchcraft had killed her.

Sensing his mother's rage at Beatriz's presence, Daniel sent her into the house to fetch Maribel. "Wrap her in her mother's gown. It calms her." Begrudgingly, Elena left the yard to fetch her granddaughter.

Staring into Maribel's milk chocolate eyes, Elena felt some relief. The girl, after all, still possessed her mother's beauty. Only she'd been damned by a jealous, cruel woman while still in her mother's womb. Not only born with a shocking addition, Maribel's disfigurement had literally scared her mother to death. Elena worried that losing her mother, especially a mother like Carmen, might become an unsurpassable tragedy for little Maribel.

As Daniel requested, Elena wrapped baby Maribel inside her mother's gown, which still carried her honeysuckle scent. Maribel cooed from within her Abuela's embrace, her third arm awkwardly hanging over the back of Elena's forearm. Elena tucked in the third arm, but, like a spring, the arm popped over the blanket, as if it had a mind of its own, as if it were saying, *I refuse to be a secret.*

This was Maribel's debut. Elena gently tucked the arm in the crook of her elbow. She felt the forceful nudging, but Maribel herself couldn't have been more content. In fact, she had yet to let out one unhappy cry. She'd come into the world only grateful to be alive. It saddened Elena that someday the child would become aware of how unlucky she really was.

Elena walked steadily into the backyard, hesitant and sad, her bare feet depending on the earth with every anxious step. Immediately, onlookers stood on their tiptoes and craned their necks. They'd heard only that Carmen had died giving birth. They knew nothing of Maribel's third arm.

As Elena approached, Daniel reached for the bundle with pride. Elena's grip was firm, but eventually, she gave in to her son, who took Maribel in his arms with absolute love. Elena's heart raced. *Be watchful*, she thought. *Beware of that wicked arm.*

But Daniel did no such thing. Instead, he raised his daughter high above his head. Carmen's gown slipped down past Maribel's belly, exposing her tiny, flailing arms, as her third arm, larger and bolder than the other two, reached even higher, making sure to be noticed.

The crowd gasped. Some women and children began to cry, and others closed their eyes. But a few—mind you, a very select few—managed to smile and blow her kisses.

"This is my daughter, Maribel, and she is a miracle," Daniel announced.

But Elena kept her eye on Beatriz Fabo, who was desperately trying to quiet her suspiciously beautiful yet obviously unhappy child. In fact, it seemed that Sammy's lungs were about to explode. He wailed like a wounded soldier. Daniel continued introducing Maribel, whom he had named Maribel Carmen Elena Trozco on the day of her birth, the third of March.

Daniel lowered his daughter and held her close to his chest and, for the first time since she was born, deliberately examined his daughter's third arm—even put the fingers to his lips and gave it a kiss. At this, Elena looked away.

Some sighs of disgust and mild terror saturated the air. But between the loss of the beloved Carmen Trozco and the arrival of this strange but mostly beautiful creature, the crowd could only defer to the topic of food.

Half the visitors stayed for the banquet that Elena had stayed up till morning preparing. She thanked Jesus that Maribel had slept through the night—a rare, miraculous occurrence for a newborn. *You strange, little beast,* Elena thought.

One particular visitor knew better than to enter the Trozco home. Beatriz Fabo stood with her back to the front door, moving her body every which way in hopes of quieting her baby. While Daniel occupied himself with Maribel, and guests piled their plates with empanadas and tamales, Elena quietly slipped outside to face Beatriz at last.

"Such an unhappy, but beautiful child," Elena said, raising her eyebrows.

"He did not sleep last night, not even an hour. I did not sleep," Beatriz mentioned quietly, the skin around her eyes forming deep, dark and wrinkled valleys of flesh.

"Be certain, Beatriz, that I will protect Maribel from you all the days of my life," Elena threatened.

"Be certain, Elena," Beatriz said, "that I will do the same for my son."

This took Elena by surprise. How dare she imply any wrongdoing on Elena's part?

"Do you think me a fool? Carmen is dead, her daughter deformed, and your baby..." Elena stared down at Sammy's face, truly the face of an angel, but an angel in hell and her heart ached.

"My child screams in pain! My child doesn't sleep! You are an awful woman, Elena! To take such violence out on an innocent child!"

It was all too much for Elena. Not only had she lost Carmen, but her granddaughter had been cursed by this frightful woman.

"Get out! Get out and never return! Curse you, you hideous woman!"

"Mama!" Daniel shouted, holding Maribel as closely as before.

"See, Daniel? This witch, your mother!" Beatriz accused, while near tears.

Daniel approached her with pity, understanding his mother's nature to think the worst developed over years of self reliance and revelation.

Elena Trozco had long been known for two things: her cooking and her temper. Never mind that she had also been widowed when her son Daniel was not yet one, when a train devoured then spit out her husband into so many pieces that his blood rained over the pale gray dirt a mile in every direction. Never mind that she alone had raised her son without the help of family, church or benevolent friends. Elena didn't have friends. It was not that she was in any way devoid of kindness or compassion; it was that her presence was so formidable the ground shook when she so much as tiptoed upon it.

Elena was what people refer to as a handsome woman. Not beautiful, not pretty, not homely, but handsome. She had a cocoa brown complexion and a face as round as the moon. Her eyes were black with subtle hints of navy blue, the eye color she was rumored to have had at birth. She wore her thick, black hair in a long, low knotted. Her lips were thin and dark, her smile more of a smirk and her body full and round. Her breasts hung like ripe pears, contained in cotton blouses often sewn from old sheets and pillow cases. She didn't owe the world charm or beauty, simply because she'd been born a woman. She didn't owe men any apologies or compliments, either, nor did she owe them her bowed head. She didn't owe anyone anything more or less than the very truth of what she was: a stern, honest and willful woman with no time for false flattery or tedious romances.

One did not trifle with Elena Trozco. Pay her a compliment and have her stare holes in your eyes as she tried to decipher your motive. Were you trying to reconcile some secret harm you'd done to her or her family, or were you trying to charm a favor out of her? Insult or attack her, or in any way show her less respect than she deserved, and Elena Trozco would eviscerate you in a way that—rather than leaving you filled with contempt, or reducing you to a shell-shocked coward in soiled pants—you would be left transformed, even grateful. Before long, there was no one left in Elena's entire world who did not have the utmost respect for her, not a soul—with a few exceptions, rather—that didn't refer to her as *Doña* Elena. She was revered, because beneath her astute severity Elena carried with her an intense and passionate wisdom that graced young and old alike with something like a lesser transfiguration. Lesser, but no less acknowledged.

Daniel stood so close to Beatriz that Maribel's independent third arm could and did reach over and pet Sammy's head, and it was then that yet another mystery was born. Sammy Fabo cried no more. The fingers of the third hand stroked Sammy's hair until his little head—red and sweaty from crying—cooled, and his real, golden complexion returned. Within moments, his eyelids flickered and closed. At last, Sammy slept.

All three adults stood speechless after having watched Maribel's arm coax the child to sleep. But Daniel finally broke the silence. He invited Beatriz to stay and to eat. He even asked her to lay the babes side by side in the basket. Beatriz smiled, but upon looking at Elena, whose eyes were still filled with suspicion and threats, she shook her head no and quietly slipped through the gate. When she did, for the very first time, Maribel wept.

CHAPTER 2

The Doctor and the Seamstress

Despite the strange, almost lovely occurrence with baby Sammy, Elena was still convinced that Maribel had been cursed, and that the arm itself would eventually do more harm than good.

"We have to get rid of it, Daniel," Elena urged her son as he rocked his daughter back and forth, smiling. "Mark my words. No good will come of this," Elena said, this time more quietly.

But Daniel's conviction had grown stronger, too. He believed now more than ever that Maribel's arm served a greater purpose than anyone could ever imagine. He replayed the moment with Sammy Fabo in his mind over and over, and when he did, he saw no curse, only the will of God.

To put his mother's pleas to rest, Daniel finally agreed to take Maribel in to their good friend, Dr. Matos. He would go alone. He insisted.

During the hours of their absence, Elena prayed. When her prayers grew damp, Elena opened the wooden trunk Daniel had built while Carmen was pregnant, to store the baby's clothing. Each and every *curandera* had correctly predicted the baby's sex, though not one of them had foreseen the arm—or had they? These days, Elena's suspicions and superstitions were growing as fast as Maribel.

One thing that had given Elena and Carmen great joy during Carmen's pregnancy was sewing a wardrobe for Maribel. Elena enjoyed sewing by hand. Carmen used a machine and tried to convince Elena—to whom she referred to always as Doña Elena—

that doing otherwise would weaken her hands. Elena would have none of it.

Now Elena examined every little dress, every *pantalon* and *camisa* with great care. She laid them each out on the bed, using her dark, bony hands to smooth them out. Then she sat in the rocking chair, where Carmen would have been nursing Maribel, and took her tears from her pocket and sweated them through her eyes and every wrinkle of her skin. She cried because Maribel and Carmen had been cursed, and she cried because she was old and would only get older. Her hands would someday fail her, her bones, her flesh—little by little she'd be deemed useless. She cried because she had been cursed, too.

It had been a week since the funeral and still Elena had not slept. It began the night after Carmen's memorial, the same day Beatriz's baby screamed and howled. From that evening on, Elena's body resisted the bed itself. So instead, she cooked. She cooked all night, and when Daniel and Maribel awoke, they had no idea.

Daniel arrived home hours later, carrying a sleeping Maribel in his arms. Elena envied her.

Elena did not make a sound. She waited. Daniel laid Maribel to rest in her bassinet, but not before kissing her forehead. Elena watched, trying to see a clue in Daniel's face as to what news he'd received from Dr. Matos. Could the curse be removed? Would Maribel grow freely, without the burden that hung from her back? Would she wear the lovely dresses made of calico fabric and lace sewn so lovingly by her mother and Abuela?

Finally, Elena could no longer suppress her urgent curiosity.

"Well?" she asked, her face still wet, her knees aching when she stood up from the chair.

Daniel sighed. He kissed his mother on her cheek. He looked beyond her ear—through the kitchen window, towards the mailbox and the silent road—and told her.

"Nothing can be done, Mama."

Elena nodded sullenly but refused to believe nothing could be done. During another sleepless night, she took each and every dress, and sat in front of the fireplace in the kitchen with her sewing kit. She had no more time to waste on tears. She could *do* something. Maribel would wear her dresses, just as her mother and Abuela had intended.

She took scissors to the back of every blouse and dress and searched for remnants of fabric to match each garment. Then, she sewed a third sleeve or arm hole. Elena had always prided herself in her abilities to hand sew with fluidity, often boasting that she could do it blindfolded or in her sleep. But for the first time since she was a child and a beginning seamstress, Elena found that when sewing the third sleeve, she couldn't help but poke herself with the needle, and with some resignation resorted to using a thimble.

While Elena sewed, Daniel slept and dreamed. In his dream he saw Carmen, floating down from heaven, assisted by three angels. Each angel, he noticed, had not two, but three wings, the third protruding from their backs just like Maribel's arm. In the dream, Carmen put her finger to her lips as if to say, *Quiet* and Daniel nodded obediently. She knelt on the floor and peered into Maribel's basket. She reached in and cradled Maribel in her arms. Just as Daniel had done at the funeral, Carmen took the little hand from Maribel's third arm and pressed it to her lips. Then she laid her back down in her basket, where Maribel still nestled against

Carmen's silk gown. Daniel reached his arms towards Carmen. Her gait was painfully slow and the closer she came to reaching him, the harder she was to see, until finally she disappeared.

It was at this time, that Daniel, too, dug out the tears from his deep pockets and sobbed his body into convulsions. Elena heard, but she did not go to him. She allowed him his pain, his pride.

The next morning it was Abuela Elena who reached into the basket and fetched a smiling Maribel. For the first time since Maribel's birth, Elena fully accepted the child, in spite of her mysterious third arm. She knew at that moment, that no curse or spell, no hint of damnation could keep her from loving Maribel.

While Daniel continued to sleep, Elena fed her granddaughter goat's milk from a glass bottle. She'd milked the goat that very morning, in preparation. Afterward, she dressed the little girl in the last dress Carmen had sewn for her, made from a rose-printed fabric. While she had to pull two of Maribel's arms through the holes, the third arm moved independently, slipping through the third armhole without any help. Elena resisted the urge to look away.

"Beautiful, just like your mother," said Elena. The moment she spoke those words, however, she was reminded of Maribel's mother, Carmen, and how her beauty had cursed her. With Maribel still in her arms, Elena picked out some red string from her sewing kit and tied it around Maribel's right wrist. If only she'd done the same for Carmen, perhaps she would still be with them now.

For Elena remembered being a young girl and watching her mother tie a red string around her *tía* Laura's wrist before meeting distant relatives.

"You're too beautiful," Elena's mother had told Laura "*Para que no te dan mal de ojo*" she said.

Elena of course, had tried—no, begged Carmen to wear the red string. But it would be the one and only time Carmen would defy Elena. She said her child was an angel, and angels deflect human pettiness and malice. Elena chose not to argue with Carmen any further, and to simply enjoy her peaceful and loving nature.

Elena kissed Maribel's forehead and brought her to a window where she saw a blue jay perched on the gate. While Maribel's eyelids grew heavy, the third arm's little hand reached out its fingers as if wanting to capture the bird or maybe to open the gate.

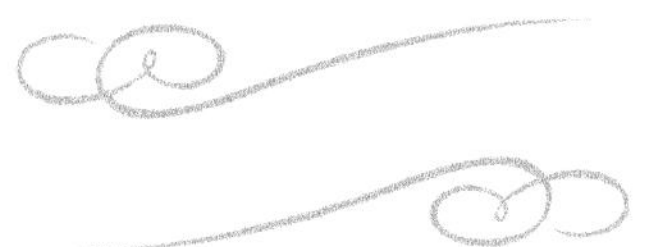

CHAPTER 3

Daniel's Deception

For the second time in his life, Daniel lied to his mother. At the age of ten, he had told his first lie. He still remembered the smell of the soap on his mother's hands before she shoved it in his mouth. He recalled how he heard the seconds ticking on the clock until Elena arrived home from the market. He expected the worst. *All this*, he'd thought, *for a pack of flat peppermint gum.*

Not only had he lied, he'd stolen. Not only had he lied and stolen, but when caught, he attempted to eat the evidence and shoved the whole pack of gum, wrappers and all, into his mouth. From that day on, not only had he not lied to his mother, he never chewed a piece of gum again. He could only think of the taste of soap in his mouth, the sound of his mother reading him John 8:44 from the Bible, telling him that Satan is the father of the lie. Daniel wanted nothing to do with the Devil. He dreamed of being a saint, being the holiest man on earth, maybe becoming a priest.

Though he lost his father, Roberto, before taking his first step, Daniel had inherited not only Roberto's striking looks, but also his gentle, altruistic nature. Dark like his mother, with the enviable bone structure of his father, Daniel's thick, wavy hair, his dominant eyebrows and full lips, his hazel eyes, made him the golden boy of the sun-beaten land where he was born and raised. His beauty, though, was more embarrassment and burden to him than it was a privilege. From the time he could speak, he prayed and he felt his words lift like a mist off his heart, rising to meet his Maker's ear, manifesting his wishes and protecting him from his fears.

As a man, Daniel stood seventy-five inches tall, towering over his mother, Elena, a woman not quite five feet in stature but a giant in presence. He was muscular and strong; a man who worked with his hands, who cut wood and dug ditches during the day and read from the Word every night. Even as a child, Daniel's first priority was knowing God and letting the Word of God sink into his being. He gave himself up to God, asking that God do with him what he like, that his life mean something, that he forgive his sinful flesh and make of him whatever he saw fit. While there were girls who left him rose-scented notes, while there were older women who examined him with anything but a mother's eye, Daniel had his heart fixed on God's plan for him. Carmen Esquivel, he would soon find out, was part of the plan he never saw coming, God's little wink, God's benevolent surprise.

Meeting Carmen introduced the obvious temptations. Although not a vixen, Carmen was absolutely enchanting and completely unaware of her charm. Both her parents had passed away when she was a young girl. Her mother had tried to have other children, but after two stillbirths, she was too broken to try again. Carmen believed this is what truly killed her parents: loss upon loss upon loss. *No human should be expected to survive such sadness,* she would often say.

Carmen bounced between *tíos* and *tías* until she was sixteen, and then she would bounce no more. She found work at a *panadería* where the owners, Lucinda and Renaldo, rented her a room that had belonged to their son who was studying abroad.

Carmen's beauty reflected her spirit. What she left behind her was a wake of kindness. She had not only changed Daniel, but Elena as well. The often stern and hostile woman that was Elena melted like chocolate in Carmen's presence. Carmen and Elena would often quote the passages of the Bible about Naomi and Ruth. When Elena refused Carmen's help, Carmen would say, "Where you go I shall go; your people will be my people."

Daniel sometimes had trouble understanding Elena and Carmen when they spoke. It seemed that his mother and wife had become so close they'd invented a language of their own. Daniel imagined sometimes that they were angels in the flesh. He was content in his fascination and needed no explanation.

He hoped now that Elena's love for him, for Carmen and now for Maribel, would enable Elena to be merciful, should she ever find out what he had done.

As promised, Daniel did in fact visit Dr. Matos. With Maribel cooing in his arms, he walked past the tobacco and liquor store, past the *panadería* where Carmen had worked, and past the *tiendas* then up the hill to the house and office of Dr. Matos. Dr. Matos, a longtime friend, was now ninety-five and nearly blind. He'd been married thirteen times. He'd fathered fifty-six children, and no one—not even Dr. Matos himself—knew how many grandchildren and great-grandchildren had come of it.

Dr. Matos had delivered both Daniel and his mother. Some folks believed he was at least one hundred and ten. But Elena always said those were *groserías*.

As always, when Daniel arrived, Dr. Matos would tell him the story of delivering Elena: that she came out not only speaking but making demands and giving orders. He said she was born with fiery red hair and blue eyes, but when her mother bathed her in buttermilk to cure her colic, Elena's eyes and skin turned mocha brown.

He would also tell Daniel the story of his birth, how he would only suckle from Elena's breast if she sang to him. She finally ran out of songs and started making up her own. She'd look around the room for inspiration and sing odd little songs about dinner plates and vases, about tables and windows. Sometimes, the songs were beautiful.

An hour into the visit, Dr. Matos finally turned his attention to Maribel. A man who'd seen more than most in his long lifetime, Dr. Matos didn't react with shock and horror at seeing her.

"Once," he told Daniel, "I delivered a baby with two heads—one coming out the top of the other."

Dr. Matos examined Maribel, and Daniel couldn't help but absorb the scene as if it were poetry. Here, this ancient man who'd delivered him and also his mother now held his baby daughter. *How the skin tells your life* Daniel thought, looking at Dr. Matos' wrinkled, rice paper skin in contrast with that of Maribel's, whose skin was flawless, as perfect as we all are in the beginning.

After reassuring Daniel that his daughter was the vision of health, he ordered X-rays. He needed to understand where the arm and Maribel overlapped or didn't, where the arm ended and where Maribel began.

When Dr. Matos left the room, it happened. Daniel saw another vision. This time, Carmen was dressed in black veils, and she wept. The three-winged angels accompanied her, singing a solemn tune.

Carmen carried a small coffin in her arms, which she laid before Daniel. The casket was open, and inside, nestled in quilted satin, laid Maribel's third arm, cold, blue, and lifeless. He looked up at Carmen and the angel, and trembled. The angels crossed their arms and shook their heads. Then, all four of them disappeared. The coffin and the arm, however, stayed just one moment longer.

While his mother had always been a cynic, Daniel Trozco had been a man who believed in signs, a mystic and a visionary. He believed this vision to be an answer to his prayers. He would not let them take Maribel's arm. *There is a reason for this*, he said softly to himself.

When Dr. Matos returned, Daniel thanked him and asked that he keep his decision about the arm confidential. Dr. Matos knew exactly what he meant: *Don't breathe a word to Elena.* Elena believed in curses, in superstitions and the selfish nature of mankind. While she considered herself a godly woman, she had no reason to believe that God would put on such "shows"—what Daniel called visions. Elena believed that God was good, but God was not a fool or a wizard for us to conjure and abandon, to blame and punish at our convenience.

Upon leaving the office with Maribel, Daniel met Beatriz Fabo halfway down the hill. Beatriz's cheeks were streaked with tears. She had always been an ugly woman, but now her ugliness garnered pity, even compassion.

In her arms she held Sammy, a boy who had grown more and more beautiful by the minute, but who cried out in agony day after day.

Daniel hoped to stop, maybe even to offer Maribel's touch once more, to see if it had been a mere coincidence or another sign of God's hand. But Beatriz downtrodden and exhausted barely had the energy to return half a smile before resuming her climb up the hill.

"Nothing can be done, Mama," Daniel had told Elena, lying to his mother for the second time in his life. But he couldn't help but think it was what God wanted. For ever since he'd lied about Maribel's arm, his mother had continued to soften in the same way she did when she first met Carmen. He could see the wholehearted acceptance in her face when she bathed Maribel, and washed her arms, all three, with equal gentleness.

It wasn't until the afternoon of the next day when Daniel worried that his lie had exacted an awful price. Elena had answered the phone, and immediately dropped to the floor, gasping.

Daniel ran to her with a whimpering Maribel in his arms.

"What is it?" he asked.

"Dr. Matos," she answered, "is dead."

CHAPTER 4
La Curandera

While the black-cloaked, wailing parade marched towards Dr. Matos' funeral, Sammy Fabo, Beatriz and Beatriz's mother, Deanna Fabo, pulled the curtains tight, as if allergic to any sliver of light. Beatriz held Sammy in her arms, Sammy whose cries had faded into whimpers. Deanna sat in her old rocking chair, the same one in which she used to rock Beatriz to sleep as a child.

When Deanna gave birth to Beatriz, she knew it would take a very special man to love her. Deana and her sisters, Luz and Soledad, spared no expense in their attempts to minimize Beatriz's unnatural homeliness. From her wardrobe, to her hair, her manicures and pedicures, they treated Beatriz like a princess, although she resembled a troll. Deanna—only a mildly attractive woman herself, who'd not had the easiest time finding the right man—wanted her daughter to have the best chance she could, working with what little to nothing she had.

Fashion and hair accessories did little to better Beatriz's aesthetic limitations. One hairdresser said it was like dressing up a mop for Sunday dinner. When hair clips and permanents, honey masks and satin dresses couldn't cut it, Deanna took Beatriz to see Magdalena Huerta, the neighborhood *curandera*.

It was rumored that Magdalena Huerta had brought a blue jay back to life while taking the life of a nasty husband who beat his poor, glassy-eyed wife. Now this beaten woman was still lonely, yes, but no longer broken. Her bruises had faded, her shattered bones had healed. Sometimes she was even seen smiling.

Some neighbors adored Magdalena, even considered her a saint. But just as many feared her, and believed her power came straight from the Devil Himself. They even claimed that she caused the fire that killed Señor and Señora Diego Castillo, as punishment for ridiculing her.

Deanna had no time or energy to squabble over the Devil and God. Her daughter's future was at stake. Whatever source granted Magdalena her power was none of Deanna's concern. On a Monday morning, when Beatriz was no more than seven years old, Deanna walked her ugly daughter to the home of Magdalena Huerta.

Approaching the door, they walked a path that cut through the middle of Magdalena's *jardín de remedios*. In her *jardín*, grew bright red ocotillo blossoms, *ponil*, agave, and *ajenjo*, as well as *tronadora*, used to treat diabetes. Beatriz squeezed her mother's left hand tighter the closer they got to the porch. Crosses hung from trees, and stone saints lined the walkway.

Before they even reached the door, Magdalena Huerta opened it and warmly invited them in. She wore nothing garish, nothing out of the ordinary as Deanna had half expected. Instead, she wore a button-up housecoat and curlers covered in a green and yellow scarf. When Magdalena turned back towards the healing room, Deanna noticed her limp and heard the alternating sound of her wooden foot scraping and then tapping against the tile floor. Magdalena was well known for pulling off her detachable wooden foot and throwing it at hoodlums who came to harass her. She had at least half a dozen replacements, and local boys who'd managed to get away with one kept it hidden somewhere sacred and deep. It was, after all, a badge of honor.

Deena shared her dilemma with Magadalena while Beatriz played in the backyard with the chickens. Magdalena shared that she'd only been approached with this particular kind of trouble one other time, and by no less of a personage than Dr. Matos himself.

"His daughter Irene had half her face torn off by a bad dog," said Magdalena. "*La pobresita* went through eight surgeries, which only succeeded in creating a stranger, more pitiful mask for the child."

"*Díos mio*" Deanna sighed. "What happened? Did you fix her?"

Magdalena shook her head, but she smiled.

"I couldn't make her pretty to everyone," Magdalena said, "but I could make her pretty to *someone*."

As it turned out, Magdalena had treated poor little Irene with a love spell, not a beauty spell. She would have to endure years of abuse and taunts at the hands of cruel children, and sometimes their even crueler parents. But on her eighteenth birthday, a man would come, and this man would find Irene to be the most beautiful woman in the whole world. He would see the true beauty of her spirit, which glowed inside of her. Under the love spell, this man would be blind to the scars, to the damage that so many years of quiet suffering had done to Irenes countenance. And just as Magdalena promised, so it happened. The man turned out to be Alfonso Escobal, a banker who had come to start a new branch in town. Alfonso was well-off and handsome. When he fell in love with Irene, people were beyond baffled. But it also changed how they saw Irene. Because he believed with all his heart that she was beautiful, those who'd known Irene all her life gradually came to see her through his eyes. They even boasted that they'd known all along she was special and destined for greatness. Liars, of course. Irene and Alfonso had been married for twenty-five years now with eleven children.

The story of Irene gave Deanna the kind of hope she hadn't felt in years.

"So you can help my little Beatriz?" she asked, her tone excited and almost giddy.

But Magdalena returned her hopefulness with a doubtful smile.

"*Mira!*" she began, "I mean no offense, Señora, but Beatriz's homeliness is more than skin deep. She has a ghost inside. Until we take out the ghost, I can do nothing."

"A ghost? What kind of crazy talk is that?" Deanna's rage nearly caused her to make a fist.

"I mean the hurt thing inside her needs to come out first. She's carrying something, something restless, something not wholehearted. She is sick to her very soul!"

"Beatriz! *Vamanos!*" Deanna yelled. She wouldn't stand for such insults. To insinuate that such a young, innocent and pitiful child, *her* child, could be haunted—it was too much to bear. She swore to herself that day she would never consult Magdalena again, even in matters of life and death.

"Señora, Señora, please, let me help you!" Magdalena called out. But Deanna grabbed her daughter around the shoulders and hurried away through the garden. She would not give up hope for Beatriz. She would find beauty for her daughter, or she would steal beauty, at any cost.

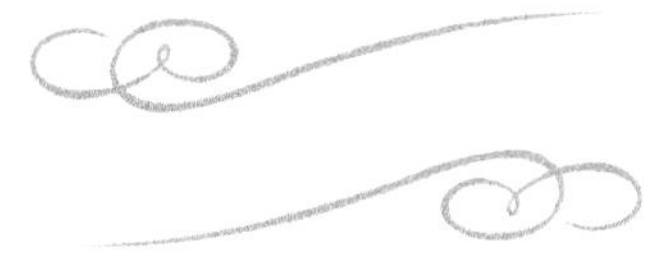

CHAPTER 5
La Tristeza de Beatriz

A man did come for Beatriz. But he did not believe she was the most beautiful woman in the world. Her homeliness simply gave his true ugliness a place to hide. This man depended on the kindness of others for drink and pity. This man was not entirely cruel, but he was entirely no good. This man had a name, but no one spoke it any longer.

One day, the man was gone. Beatriz and her mother agreed, he'd run away or he'd been killed—he was deeply in debt, borrowing from shady, unforgiving sorts. The people of the town made cruel jokes about his departure—for instance, that this man's ugliness and Beatriz's ugliness combined had killed him. Beatriz had come to expect nothing but cruelty from others. Only two people had ever surprised her with kindness: Carmen and Daniel Trozco. It was a kindness she would have to forget now that Elena Trozco was convinced that Beatriz had cursed an innocent child.

Even though Sammy's cries had finally lessened, he appeared no less miserable, as if he'd come into this world with a fear plaguing him. Beatriz's aunt Soledad was something of a *curandera* herself, though nothing in power compared to Magdalena Huerta. Soledad tried several remedies: bathing the baby in chamomile, massaging his belly button with Beatriz's breast milk, and rubbing her own saliva on his hardened belly. Beatriz wasn't sure if it was a combination of these remedies that helped her son, or if the poor child had just worn himself out. Either way, he was healing, but only in slivers.

Even through his tears and misery, Sammy's unearthly beauty captivated the people of the town. His glowing complexion promised perfection, albeit painful perfection. Soledad guarded her nephew with a plethora of spells and *remedios* to protect Sammy from the *mal de ojo*. For the Fabo family, Sammy was a dangerous hope.

Beatriz's thoughts turned to the Trozco's three-armed baby, whom Elena had accused her of cursing. She wondered if the poor child would suffer the same cruelty she had during her youth, the cruelty she still suffered from those around her. She thought about the day of Carmen's funeral and how the third arm had reached over and petted her newborn son's head. Before or since, she had never seen Sammy in such a state of calm. It was as if the arm had been searching, reaching for Sammy to soothe his pain.

Beatriz laid Sammy beside her and kissed his forehead. He smelled like warm milk and peaches. She held one of his tiny hands and put it to her cheek to caress her face. She closed her eyes and wondered what her life might be like without so much ugliness and pain.

CHAPTER 6

Child in the Mirror

Elena had no shortage of black dresses and shrouds. Most women her age had lost count of how many funerals they'd attended in their lifetimes. For Maribel, it was number two. Elena had stayed up all night sewing Maribel's first mourning dress. She couldn't help but shake her head and even give a mild laugh as she wrapped the tiny child in yards of black fabric. *How ridiculous* she thought, *that a child would be memorializing her second dead body before she cuts her first tooth!*

Daniel took Maribel in his arms before they walked out the door to meet and join the hundreds of mourners. To Elena they resembled a legion of black-shrouded ghosts. Some grieved openly, wailing and sometimes stumbling to their knees. Others sang hymns and said prayers as everyone made the solemn pilgrimage up the hill to the place where Dr. Matos had once lived and practiced medicine.

Inside the house, all the mirrors were either covered with veils or turned over, as were all pictures of the late Dr. Matos. Guests could hear the sobs coming from the private room where Dr. Matos' daughter Irene, and his most recent wife, Sonia, were grieving. The descendants of Dr. Matos were mostly easy to spot because of his dominant genes. Many of the children in the home who chased each other through hallways and under tables had his nose, or his laugh or even his serious brows. Mothers yelled at their unruly children, expecting them to understand the seriousness and grief of the occasion. But the children did not understand the absolute permanence of death. For them, every day was either a temporary dream or a nightmare that would dissolve by the following day.

It was finally Elena's turn to pay her respects. She looked down at the casket at the man who'd brought her into this world. Now that man was gone forever. She did not like to admit it, since she considered herself very religious, but Elena had doubts. She could recite promises of Heaven and life everlasting forwards and backwards, but they failed to resonate with her completely. Still she had mouthed the words of prayers and scriptures her whole life, hoping that either her doubt would die, or that the truth would sink its claws into her. Elena paid her respects to Dr. Matos, now just an elf of a man in a wooden box.

Daniel was next in line after Elena. Daniel leaned forward, Maribel in his arms, and kissed Dr. Matos' forehead. While his eyes were closed and he muttered a soft, inaudible prayer to Dr. Matos, Maribel's third arm rose from under her blanket and grabbed hold of Dr. Matos' tie. Elena felt a thick lump swell in her throat, and her face felt as though it had caught fire. Daniel, on the other hand, remained unaltered as he struggled to pry the fingers off the dead man's tie. Elena eyed the crowd, taking notice of who was squirming or giggling. *Nasty, nasty arm!* Elena thought to herself.

The hand held a firm grip, and when Daniel pulled Maribel away from the casket, the dead man rose with her. Not much, just an inch or so, but enough to draw gasps and some giggles from the crowd. In unflinching perseverance and without a trace of self-consciousness, Daniel leaned slightly into the coffin to let the body return to its position. The hand finally let go.

"Give her to me!" Elena whispered angrily to Daniel. With a sheepish smile, he handed Maribel over to his mother.

Elena couldn't be angry with her infant granddaughter, and she couldn't be angry with her saintly, loving son. But the arm, she could loathe that arm. After all, she thought, *That arm is not Maribel, and Maribel is not the arm.* Elena Trozco firmly believed the arm acted independently of Maribel. But she knew better than to share these thoughts with her son. He had faith that Maribel's infamous arm was a blessing that came with a purpose, and that purpose had everything to do with his daughter.

Elena also couldn't help but find Beatriz Fabo's absence at the funeral significant. Elena's interest intensified when she overheard a conversation between a woman Elena thought she recognized from the post office and one of the granddaughters Dr. Matos had had working as his receptionist. There had been so many, Elena could not remember her name.

"He was old, yes, very old." She spoke softly. "But I had just seen Papí that morning and he was so full of life, doing his morning sit-ups and jumping jacks. He had two appointments in the afternoon, but he didn't want me to stay. I thought it was strange the next day, when I found him and one of the charts from the day before still lay on his desk."

"Whose was it?" the woman asked.

"I don't know if I should say," the granddaughter said as she looked over her shoulder. She didn't notice that the Trozco matriarch listened under a fragile shadow in the corner, "If I tell you, you can't tell anyone else. Do you understand?"

"Yes, yes!" the guest responded.

"Beatriz. That is, her son, Sammy. Something was wrong with him." The granddaughter spoke quietly, but Elena had trained her ears for such occasions.

"*Por díos,*" sighed the guest. "Do you think...what?"

The granddaughter shook her head.

"But who came first? Who was the first visitor?"

The granddaughter shrugged her shoulders. She did not know.

Just then, it hit Elena. It had to have been Daniel. Her son and granddaughter were two of the last people on this earth to have seen Dr. Matos alive. But Beatriz, she thought, Beatriz was the very last.

She squeezed Maribel closer to her bosom to warm the chill she felt go down her spine. Daniel often chided her for her superstitions, especially those suspicions held against Beatriz Fabo. Carmen had done the same when she was alive. But Elena knew there was something no good about Beatriz. As her thoughts delved deeper and deeper into suspicion and loathing, she felt a sharp pinch on her forearm. She jumped a little, and then quickly recovered. It was the arm again, the third arm that left a bright pink star from the pinch. That's when Elena entertained the craziest thought of all: Could the arm read her mind?

Two small boys raced through the room. They were playing a game, turning all the mirrors over as two women with graying hair chased after them, one with a wooden spoon and the other with a belt. One boy rushed past either side of Elena and knocked over an end table where one mirror had sat. With Maribel in her arms, Elena carefully squatted down to turn the mirror over. What she saw made her scream and gave her so much fright that she dropped the mirror, and it shattered. As she leaned over the mirror, in the place where the arm protruded from Maribel's back, she saw a face instead. It was another child altogether. The face was wet with tears, the eyes a deep purple, the hair auburn.

"Señora Trozco!" One of Dr. Matos' grandsons came to her rescue and helped her back to her feet and guided her into a soft armchair. He was asking her questions, but she couldn't hear a thing. Instead she turned her granddaughter over, investigating each one of her arms, in search of the phantom child. But all that she found were the pieces of Maribel that were always there, including *that arm*. All the jostling woke Maribel, and Daniel offered to take her back. Elena returned her without a word.

"Mama? What's wrong?" he asked.

"*Nada, nada,*" she said and insisted that they go home.

The light outside was dying, and without the light, the black figures in mourning might disappear into the dark without a trace.

CHAPTER 7
Coco

Three years had passed since the day of Dr. Matos' funeral, and since then, Maribel had not had any occasion to wear her funeral frock. Instead, she wore red every day she could. Maribel lived in the color red. She ate strawberries ripe and red, picked the reddest of roses, and she chose the reddest of apples that her father brought home from a day in the orchards.

Abuela Elena often told Maribel that she loved the color red so much because of her heart. She told Maribel her heart was the reddest heart in the entire world because it was filled with so much *cariño*. Elena often believed Maribel to be the happiest child in the entire world because of that deliciously red heart.

It was true, Maribel couldn't be happier. Sammy Fabo, however, was a different story. His quiet, sad beauty left a thick cloud of resigned sorrow behind him everywhere he went. However, in the presence of Maribel—or maybe more importantly, Coco, the name Maribel had given her third arm—Sammy was able to throw the black cloud over his shoulder.

Though Elena's suspicions regarding Beatriz Fabo hadn't lessened, Sammy's affection for Maribel and Maribel's joyful effect on Sammy had sparked her compassion to allow regular, almost daily play dates between Maribel and Sammy. After all, Elena also had a red, red heart too, the heart of an *abuela*, and she couldn't deny happiness to such a melancholy child.

So Maribel and Sammy played in sand and water, they mixed the *masa* for Elena's tamales, they cut paper and folded the squares into cranes. Each day, Beatriz waited by the gate to pick up her son. She nodded towards Elena in recognition of her specific kindness and smiled at lovely Maribel, who waved at her with all three arms.

It might have happened many times without anyone noticing, but it first came to Elena's notice at her son Daniel's twenty-fifth birthday. Sammy and Maribel were frosting some *pasteles* and Elena watched them closely to make sure they weren't eating more than they were frosting. That's when she heard the name Coco.

"Mari, Mari, Coco wants help!" Sammy shouted.

"Shhh, Sammy! Okay. Here, Coco, you have green. Sammy, take yellow and I get red."

When Maribel's third arm wiggled excitedly before picking up the green frosting, Elena nearly fainted. It wasn't enough that her granddaughter would have to live the rest of her life with this deformity, but now she had given it a name?

Hard as she tried to avoid the subject of the third arm with Daniel, Elena finally came to him with the news. Elena felt that naming the extra arm only gave it more power. But Daniel let out a small laugh and only said, "Coco, hmm...Coco. *Me gusta*!"

"Coco says '*hola,*' Papí!" Maribel shouted out at her father after overhearing him.

Elena gave him the look, the look that said that if it weren't for the obvious discrepancy in their sizes and strength, she would take him over her knee and spank him till his bottom went numb.

"Abuelita," Maribel cried, "Coco love Papí. Coco love Sammy. Coco love me."

It came as no surprise to Elena that Maribel said nothing about Coco's affection for her.

"Hmmph," Elena snorted.

Though she tried to discourage her granddaughter from personalizing and empowering her worrisome deformity, Elena resigned herself to the reality: Maribel had acknowledged Coco's will, and there was no going back. Elena had also learned an important lesson when raising Daniel—one that most mothers come to realize: The harder you try to pull a child one way, the harder they pull in the other direction. Someone has to give in, or both of you will fall.

Plus, Elena couldn't complain. Better to have Maribel full of joy, embracing her light spirit, than stumbling sadly like that poor ghost of a boy, Sammy Fabo.

Maribel had not yet started school, and already her circle of friends was growing. Aside from her true-blue Sammy, Maribel made friends with three other girls in the neighborhood. Lucita was four, Normita was three like Maribel, and Carmelita, the oldest of them all, was five. The little girls had no qualms inquiring about the third arm.

Maribel said, "I call it Coco, but Abuelita doesn't like that."

"I want a Coco!" Normita shouted, followed by, "Me too! Me too!" from the two other girls.

Lucita even asked, "Mari, can you fly?"

Maribel looked down and shook her head. She turned around and pulled down her skirt and underwear to show the girls her bruised bottom. Maribel herself had wondered the same thing. She'd tried jumping off fence posts and ladders.

"Does it hurt, Marrriii?" Normita asked, with half her thumb still in her mouth.

"No. Coco doesn't hurt."

The three girls circled Maribel's back and inspected Coco. Coco had grown to be less hardy and thick, and more sleek, like the arm of a mannequin. The little girls took turns beautifying and adorning Coco. Lucita painted her nails yellow and orange. Carmelita dressed Coco's wrist in silver bracelets. Normita painted flowers and hearts up to her elbow. All the while, Maribel continued on in her own play. She frosted the *pasteles*, sometimes licking some of the red icing from her fingers. She was content to occupy herself and happy that her friends kept Coco company. She wouldn't mind if her friends came to love Coco as much as they loved her. Her heart was a deep red.

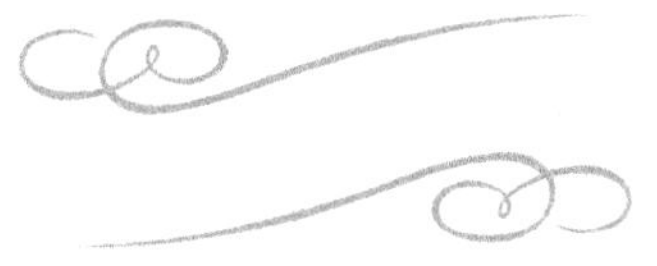

CHAPTER 8
The Sullen Boy

There's a reason why you don't stare directly into the sun and why you protect your eyes during an eclipse. Regardless of how beautiful, how awe inspiring it might be, beauty, when it borders on the supernatural, can blind us.

Sammy Fabo was such a beauty, and if it weren't for the fact that his beauty was tempered with a palpable sadness, he, too, could have brought onlookers to their knees. At first glance strangers would say, while holding back tears of amazement, "What a child! What a beautiful child!" To call him beautiful was an understatement, and the moment the word was spoken, a bashful smear of red crossed the faces of his admirers. Sammy was a golden-skinned boy with green eyes that lit up like stars and hair that matched the most luminous stalks of wheat at sunset. His teeth were little pearls and his rose-colored lips a heart-shaped blossom framed by jewel-like dimples upon his glowing cheeks.

However, before long, everyone felt it. Some would even whisper, "Something is not quite there." One could only stand in the shadow of Sammy Fabo's beauty for so long before feeling the sting of his mysterious void, his colorless heart.

He was a painfully shy and quiet child, too. The extra attention to his deliciousness only made things worse. For the first time in Sammy's mother's life, Beatriz was grateful for her lack of beauty. For when things got to be too much for Sammy, Beatriz stepped in, proudly displaying her face like a scorpion does her tail, until she put strangers off and they left them both alone. Of course, to Sammy, his mother was neither beautiful nor hideous—she was only Mother, she was Creator, she was above all Love. He cherished her deeply.

Though he felt his mother's love for him, though it comforted him in times of illness and during certain waves of fear, it was no cure for his chronic melancholy. The only cure for that was Maribel Trozco, the girl with three arms.

It never occurred to Sammy that Maribel should only have two arms. In fact, why not four? Why not six? What difference did it make? In Maribel, Sammy found light—but, no, more than that, he had with Maribel a respite from persistent heartache, from the empty cave in his chest. Perhaps he'd discovered in her something brand new, something no one else in the world had ever experienced and therefore no word existed for it yet. Maybe it was the world's freshest invention of delightful, magical things.

CHAPTER 9

Daniel and Beatriz

What Elena Trozco did not know—though she knew a great many things—was that Beatriz Fabo loved Daniel, Elena's only son. She did not know that the day after Dr. Matos' funeral—some three years ago—Beatriz had revealed to Daniel the mystery of Dr. Matos' death.

Elena did not know that an exhausted, all but hopeless, Beatriz Fabo had climbed the steep hill to Dr. Matos' home and office with her whimpering child in her arms, that she presented her broken-hearted son to Dr. Matos, and how Dr. Matos held him and began to cry. He cried so much it looked like rain, and Sammy's blanket soaked up the old man's tears.

Dr. Matos said, "So much sadness in this poor child. So much! It's not right."

Eventually, Dr. Matos began to shudder, and his slight, ancient self doubled over in hysterical sobs. Beatriz reached for her child, but Dr. Matos shook his head and held on.

"It isn't right," he repeated.

Finally his crying stopped, and beneath him a puddle of tears circled the three of them, a lake of sorrow.

Dr. Matos kissed Sammy on each cheek and on the forehead before returning him to his mother. That's when it happened.

"And just like that? He died?" Daniel had asked her.

"*Sí*. He took the brunt of Sammy's sadness upon himself. Not all of it, obviously, but enough to keep Sammy here with me. If he hadn't, Sammy would have died of a broken heart instead of Dr. Matos."

"He did the right thing," Daniel had said, trying to comfort her. "He lived a long, long, happy life."

Elena Trozco did not know that this conversation between her son and Beatriz Fabo was just the first of many that would take place over the next three years. Elena had no idea that when Daniel gathered wood or milked the goats, he always took enough not just for his family but for the Fabo women as well. It was a home without men, and Sammy was but the promise of a man.

Elena had no idea that over those past three years, her son had actually visited Beatriz every single day if only for a minute. At first it was out of pity and because he knew it was what Carmen would have wanted. The child needed a man in his life, and he felt the women could certainly use his help and generosity. But as time passed and visits added up like sands of karma and fate, Daniel no longer found a single flaw upon Beatriz's soft and smiling face. Was it her mouth? Her nose? Her ears? Was it her smile? The truth was that all Daniel saw when he searched Beatriz's face were features and parts that made up every face in the world. He could no longer grasp what made one woman beautiful and another homely.

Elena didn't know any of it. Elena couldn't know, should never know.

One woman knew too much, and that woman was Beatriz's own mother, Deanna Fabo. Deanna knew about Daniel and Beatriz's secret friendship. She knew what had really happened to Carmen. She knew why her grandson was born with melancholy. She had stolen beauty. Her child and grandchild would pay the price.

CHAPTER **10**

Beatriz and Carmen

Before there was a Maribel or a Sammy, there was a beautiful goddess of a girl named Carmen Esquivel. Carmen was only sixteen years old when she began working at the *panadería*. Life had at times scolded and throttled Carmen, it's true, but miraculously it had left no marks. Carmen had blue-black hair that she often wore in two braids joined at the top like a crown. Sometimes she wore tiger lilies on the top of her head. She wore a mango print orange and green apron. Her hands were darker than the rest of her. Her hazel eyes and rose-lipped smile greeted each patron with the same cheerful openness, a loveliness that summoned magic.

Two of her most regular patrons were Deanna and Beatriz Fabo. Beatriz usually walked in with downcast eyes, her hand trapped it seemed inside her mother's grip. She knew their order before they spoke; two *conchas* for Beatriz, an empanada and *puerquito* for Deanna. Carmen couldn't help but notice Beatriz's distance and how she wouldn't allow herself to look anyone in the eye. Carmen felt an ugly scratching at her heart every time she saw Beatriz staring down at her shiny shoes.

Beatriz, Carmen thought, was much like her first tray of *elotes*. Inside the sugar-sprinkled, horn-shaped pastry was a delicious cookie-like filling. But the outside was overcooked, had lost its shape. No one would eat them, save her and a few neighborhood children. Beatriz had lost her shape because the wrong people were molding her. Inside her was something worth knowing. Carmen even caught herself being proud that she might be the only person in town who knew this about Beatriz. Inwardly, she reprimanded herself for her pride.

Little by little, with each of their visits, Carmen commented on something that Beatriz was wearing, as she always came adorned in the latest fashions, high-priced silks and hairstyles. Some awful men who also frequented the *panadería* would often mock her, saying she was God's joke to men, because from behind she looked like such a princess, but when they saw her face it cursed their eyes. Carmen was often tempted to reserve some empanadas full of eggshells for those men, but she knew better. Something had poisoned them when they were young; someone taught them the wrong way and it wasn't up to her, but to God to serve them their medicine.

After weeks of visits from the Fabo women and dozens of *panes dulces* later, Carmen caught her first glimmer of hope. It was brief and subtle, and to anyone else it would have gone unnoticed. But Carmen was determined to get to the center of Beatriz Fabo, so she closely studied her every gesture, no matter how minimal.

It happened quickly, probably so Deanna wouldn't notice and also because perhaps Beatriz would have lost her nerve otherwise. But as she turned away from the counter and Carmen sang as she did each time, "God bless you and yours," Beatriz pulled out two roses, one yellow, one red, from her pocket and sat them on the counter. She still didn't look Carmen in the eye when she walked out the door, but before the door shut, Carmen thought she noticed a slight smile on Beatriz's face.

When Carmen touched the roses, she found that they were made of silk, and on the back of each rose, Beatriz had sewn a hair clip. Carmen swelled with joy and wore the clips in her hair the very next day. But the Fabos did not come in. She wore them the day after that, and after that, and after that, and still they didn't come.

Carmen worried that something had happened to them. She especially worried about Beatriz. Though she tried never to judge others, she couldn't help but feel a chill when Deanna Fabo neared her. When money changed hands and Deanna's hand brushed against Carmen's, she felt a sick, twisting pain in her gut.

When they finally returned, it was obvious something had changed. Deanna appeared less hostile. She carried with her an air of self-satisfaction that replaced her former coldness.

Beatriz, on the other hand, with her gray dress and hooded coat, appeared more withdrawn than ever. It was as if the moment with the rose hair clips had never happened. Somehow, Beatriz had taken not one but several steps back, farther away from Carmen than before.

"Señorita," Deanna Fabo greeted Carmen, "*Perdon*, but there has been a terrible mistake."

Deanna delivered the line with a transparent smile.

"Oh? Is that why you haven't been back? Was it the *conchas*? The empanadas?"

"No, no, *linda,*" Deanna spoke, "I'm afraid the mistake was on our part. I see you are wearing the roses my daughter Beatriz gave you on our last visit?"

"Oh, *sí por supuesto,* they are so beautiful." Carmen hoped her words of praise were reaching Beatriz's ears. "So kind of you."

"*Sí*, yes they are. But I'm afraid they were not Beatriz's to give away. They were made by my sister, Soledad. She means to sell them at the *mercado*. If you like them you can visit her table this Saturday. But I will need those back, *lo siento.*"

Carmen caught Beatriz shifting a little when Deanna spoke. She also thought she could hear Beatriz grinding her teeth, the angry kind of grinding you feel in your ribs when you are unjustly silenced.

"Oh, *por cierto*," Carmen reached her hand to the top of her head and gently pulled the yellow and red roses out of her hair, pulling out a few strands in the process.

Before she could put them on the counter, Deanna's hungry hand reached out and took them from her.

"*Mucho perdon,* Señorita," Deanna said to Carmen, "*Gracias.*"

"Yes, of course, Señora Fabo."

Carmen forced herself not to look in Beatriz's direction. Beatriz's shame and sorrow grew fingers, softly touching Carmen's face. She would not add to it.

The two Fabo women left without ordering, but they would be back. With each visit, Carmen desperately tried to regain the small bit of progress she'd made with Beatriz; with her smile, her compliments, her invitation—albeit quiet and subtle—of friendship. *Nada.*

Before too long, it was Daniel Trozco who wandered into the *panadería,* Daniel who received and returned her smiles and her invitation. Before too long, she would marry him. She would become Carmen Trozco.

Beatriz, however, shut herself off in her bedroom sewing her own flowers from red and yellow silk.

CHAPTER 11

The Paper Girl

By the time she turned ten, Maribel had her own definitive style. She kept her blue-black hair cropped in a bob right below the ears, with blunt bangs. She wore red cardigans and red tights. She often wore dresses with polka dots or flower-printed summer dresses. Elena was the seamstress but Maribel was the designer.

Maribel hummed little melodies from songs she'd managed to remember from her infancy. She walked with the precision of a dancer and spoke through cheerful smiles. When she laughed, angels laughed with her.

Maribel's most notable gift, however, was her ability to breathe life into folded paper. Even as a toddler, her affinity for folding paper hats with Sammy seemed to foreshadow a greater talent. Over the years, the complexity of Maribel's designs and the sophistication of her creatures evolved, growing into a compelling collection that often left visitors sighing in awe. Maribel's creations hung from the ceiling, the slightest draft or gust of air fully animating their wings, their necks, their legs. Once she'd filled her bedroom, she began to fill the dining room, the living room, the kitchen and even the bathroom.

Above the dining room table was her most sophisticated creation: a mobile-like chandelier made of glossy paper in multiple colors and shades folded into a menagerie of circus performers and animals. The first time Elena laid eyes on the masterpiece, she thought to herself, *My strange beautiful nieta, she can breathe life into anything.*

No one could be more aware of this than Sammy Fabo. The older Sammy grew, the less his melancholy weighed. It was as if Maribel had folded bits of his sadness into cranes and sent them off into the blue where all quiet and haunted things belong. Maribel and Coco had saved him from death by heartbreak, so Sammy doted on them both.

Maribel's father, Daniel, explained to her that Abuela Elena's heart had rearranged itself, squeezing the anger and resentment she felt toward Beatriz Fabo to the very bottom of her heart, while making room to love Sammy entirely. He'd become something of a second grandchild to her. Like so many others, Elena was taken by Sammy's beauty, but more than that, Elena knew that the best gift she could give to anyone in this world was the absence of pain. Sammy had peace as long as he had Maribel.

While Maribel had always loved her Abuela Elena, it was around this age that Maribel truly fell in love with her, the way little girls fall in love with the image of Woman they themselves aspire to become one day—the very ideal of feminine power and strength. It was the little things: the care Elena took in braiding Maribel's hair before school, the way Elena came into her room every night and pulled the curtains shut, how the kiss she left on Maribel's forehead tingled like a blessing, lastly, how Elena made room for Coco, even though Maribel knew that Elena would wish Coco away forever if she could.

It was obvious to Maribel, through her *abuela* Elena's eyes and the tightness in her lips when she came into contact with Maribel's third arm, that Elena despised Coco. Maribel had planned on many occasions to tell her about Coco, to really explain what Coco meant to her, to everyone. But because her beloved abuela lifted the moon onto her shoulders, because she placed it inside Maribel's window each and every night, Maribel couldn't bear to share anything distasteful with her.

Instead, it was Maribel and Maribel alone who sometimes bore the dead weight of a despondent Coco who slept when she wanted to be at play and fidgeted at times when Maribel only wanted slumber.

Some children are innately blessed with the ability to understand in an almost severe—and at the very least, adult way—what is to be shared and what is to be concealed. Maribel possessed this ability along with her many other talents. Because of this, Maribel knew better than to explain Coco to her abuela, and, just as importantly, why she knew not to mention the relationship between her father and Beatriz Fabo. Daniel had been nervous at first, to involve his daughter in these clandestine visits. Not only that, but he wanted to give Sammy his full, undivided attention when he could. He knew the boy had a big hole in his heart, like that of an old man who's outlived all his kin. He wanted to fill it with a fatherly kind of love. It was only when Beatriz finally asked him that he started bringing Maribel. After all, Beatriz noticed that as beautiful as Daniel's intentions were, the hole in Sammy's heart was a Maribel-shaped void that she alone could fill.

Their second concern, of course, was Sammy. Sammy was a very different sort of child than Maribel. He was fragile, sometimes insecure. Rather than rely on threats or fear in order to keep the boy from divulging their secret, they put their faith in Maribel and her example. It was a reckless faith they had, but they were desperate to believe that they could keep their friendship turned affair a secret from Elena Trozco.

As it turned out, Sammy's own demeanor—somber, quiet, and withdrawn—served them well. When Sammy needed or wanted anything, he whispered it into Maribel's ear and she translated his request. Maribel could see how her father lit up when he visited the Fabo household, how Beatriz appeared a little less gray, less muted. As Maribel grew older, she began to understand the true nature of her father and Beatriz's relationship. She could almost make out the red thread that connected their two hearts together. Sometimes, as she watched them exchanging delicate, blushing looks, she would draw the thread in the air with her forefinger. Daniel would ask her, "What are you doing, sweet girl?"

"Drawing the love," Maribel would say.

Sometimes she drew the thread going between their two hearts, other times she'd stretch that thread to her and to Sammy. It was because of this love that Maribel also kept a secret from her father.

In the beginning, it was a minor annoyance. But over the years, as Maribel grew into a little lady-shaped girl, the dismissible ache turned into full-blown pain, sometimes even agony. It was Coco. Inside the Fabo household, Coco felt much heavier, like a dead weight that pulled at Maribel's back so much so she had to hunch over, pulling her arms out and up in front of her torso. In order to not cause panic to anyone, Maribel walked and stood as little as possible when visiting the Fabos. Instead she sat with her back, and the seemingly comatose Coco, up against the wall or the couch.

While the forbidden flames between Beatriz and Daniel were enough to keep them distracted and unaware of Maribel's cumulative suffering, there was nothing that stayed hidden from Deanna Fabo.

"What troubles you, child?" she would ask.

It was in these moments, when Deanna Fabo hovered over Maribel with a smile half revealing bitterness and half concern, that Coco ached hardest, pulling at Maribel's spine.

"Nothing, Doña Deanna. *Estoy bien*," Maribel offered. And while she wasn't a dishonest child, something told her that Deanna Fabo's interest in her, and, more likely, in Coco, wasn't completely benevolent.

"Are you sure, child?" This is when Deanna Fabo would put her hand on Maribel's head, and the lightest touch seemed to set

Coco on fire with pain—a pain Maribel shared and yet had to do everything to bury and conceal.

Maribel knew the time was near, and she felt inside her red, red heart that, Deanna did, too.

CHAPTER **12**

The Writing on the Wall

Sometimes I wish I could live both lives at once. In one life, I will stay quiet and good and I will not let the secrets creep their way out of me. I will not let them know, especially the children. I will carry my own weight. But in the other life, I rage. I say why I am made this way, and the men and women and children are scared. And the men and women and children yell. And the men and women and children cannot understand how it happened and how they made me so, so incomplete.

I was to be a child, too. I was to be the child less beautiful, and I was to be the lesser child, but I would have been happy, don't you think? I would have been born with a body and legs. My legs would walk me to parks and swimming holes, to outdoor markets where fresh bread is sold. But that is the third life, the life when I am whole. I am not whole, though. I am me, and I choose between the quiet life and the raging life.

But then I came up with this: the in-between life, the middle path. So I write this to you on your wall, and I write to you because you are the closest thing to being whole and the best of the people I know. I don't want to scare you, little girl, I just want you to understand that I won't always be a part of you. I can't. See, I was a part of someone else, and something bad separated us, and something good gave me someone else to be a part of: you.

You have been kind, and you have been good. But maybe once you know what I really am, you will be afraid, and you'll want to cut me away! I can't let you do that, though. I can't let you destroy me, when destroying me might destroy him. The thing is, I am suffering a great deal more lately than ever. No, it isn't because of you, it is because of the bad thing that was done long before you were born or he was born. It is because people take things they shouldn't. You know who, don't you? You can feel it when she is near. You can feel me turn rock hard, then numb, then full of rage. I don't mean to hurt you, little thing. If I had become a child, I could have made her understand the curse of it all.

Are you beginning to understand? Have I been too vague? I am afraid. I know I am not a whole child, but I am still afraid of disappearing before my time. Do you see?

Before you gave me a name, there were other names for me, like Spirit or Ghost. But then you gave me the name, and I need to thank you for that, Maribel. I do love my name. Before you gave me the name, I was apt to turn into darkness. I mean not only that I would turn to darkness, but I would have become Darkness itself. That's what happens, you see, when people think they know better, when a person destroys the spirit of a child, and destroys the home that spirit belongs to: the spirit must find another place to be born into.

I still remember the day I was broken. The panadería *where the beautiful girl worked. Your mother! Your mother, Maribel! Oh what a horror, what a tragedy you never knew her. She was a saint, a beautiful saint. I believe I loved her or could have loved her. I believe we could have been friends. She was kind, like your father is kind, like you are kind. I try to be kind. Sometimes I manage. Other times the darkness holds me hard.*

Carmen would have been my kindred spirit. But she *could not let it happen. I was* hers. *I had to be hers. Don't you see? When the spirit of a child is broken, that spirit must reach out and find another home. You are my home. But you won't be my house forever. I need to return to my home—my real home, Maribel. I need to return to that broken heart and fill the gaps of my girl home once again. Are you beginning to understand? Beatriz. I need Beatriz. Otherwise, Sammy, he will suffer. Yours, Coco*

That morning, Maribel woke up and read the long letter from Coco, scrawled sideways, as she'd written it while Maribel slept on her side with her back to the wall. Maribel rose from her bed as though it were any other morning. But this day she grabbed a bucket filled with warm water and soap. She scrubbed the wall clean after memorizing every word of Coco's plea. She dressed, made her bed, and didn't tell a single soul.

CHAPTER 13
Elena's Sleepless Night

As a special treat for both children, from time to time Elena allowed Sammy to sleep over. If the night was especially warm, Elena would allow Maribel and Sammy to sleep outside in a tent lovingly constructed by Daniel. Although the children believed they were camping outside all on their own, it was often the case that Daniel slept in a hammock between two trees just a few yards from the children. This delighted Elena for several reasons. Sammy and Maribel were only children, no siblings to grow up with, no brothers or sisters to sing silly songs with, to laugh with, and even to fight with. In the Trozco home, Elena had built a part-time family for each child, complete with a mother and Abuela figure in her, and a father figure in Daniel.

Elena found in her old age that she was even softening, just slightly, towards Beatriz, although she vowed to anyone who would listen that she would never forgive Beatriz for cursing her family. On Sundays after church, she often sent surplus cornbread and apples to the Fabos' home with Sammy. Though she still did not allow Beatriz or any Fabo other than Sammy to enter her home, she sometimes felt something delicate sweep over her bruised heart when Beatriz came to pick Sammy up from play dates. What she saw in Beatriz was a woman mostly defeated yet desperately in love with her sullen child. What she saw was the glorious thing only one loving mother recognizes in another.

It was a Friday night when this particular sleepover took place. That night, Maribel had created another paper wonder, one of herself and Sammy holding hands. It had taken her hours, and it was obvious to Elena there was something very special about this particular work of art. She noticed her granddaughter often took deep breaths and arched her back, even watched her wince in pain from time to time.

"Mari, qué te pasa?" She would ask.

But Maribel insisted, *"Nada,* Abuelita," and she'd beam a brilliant, reassuring smile in Elena's direction.

That night, Daniel built the children a fort out of painted cardboard boxes and tarpaulin. He gave them each a lantern so they wouldn't fear the dark. Elena brought the children *churros* and hot chocolate with cinnamon, Sammy's favorites. Maribel finished the paper versions of herself and Sammy and hung them from the ceiling of the great big box her father had arranged for them. It was a night like so many others, and yet, what followed would be a morning like no other.

Elena had tried a myriad of tricks and spells to abate the insomnia over the years, but nothing helped. For a while, she'd been in the practice of counting every loved one and not so loved one she'd buried in her lifetime. Some nights, she'd put them in order by year of death; other nights, she'd put them order by age at death. It was morbid, yes, but she found it strangely comforting to remember the dead, and she often wondered what type of sleep death would bring her.

The night of the most recent sleepover, however, while Sammy and Maribel's lanterns slowly began to fade, Elena wandered from room to room, absorbing the magnitude of Maribel's menagerie. Over the years, the ceilings and walls had showcased the paper zebras and giraffes, lions and doves, cranes and frogs. It was only recently that Maribel had shifted her focus to people. Elena smiled, though weary with exhaustion, when she walked into the sun room, and looked up at the paper mobile that Maribel had given her for *Día de las Madres*. In the center was the moon, covered in silver glitter, and from the moon hung an origami sculpture in Elena's likeness and in her arms she held baby Maribel, notably sans Coco. It was on this very night, at this very moment, that Elena truly absorbed the meaning of Coco's absence from Maribel's creation: Maribel knew full well of Elena's severe distaste for Coco. Elena realized, with something just short of horror, that her granddaughter excluded Coco from this gift out of full awareness that her Abuela resented, even hated something that was part of her, attached to her since birth and even before that.

"*Ay, Díos mío,*" Elena lamented quietly to herself.

Elena took a few minutes to gather herself, then she walked out onto the patio, past the garden to the lawn where the children slept in their cardboard fortress. Her son, Daniel, slept peacefully in the hammock nearby. She gathered the empty mugs and peeked in on the children. They slept side by side, holding hands, while above them Maribel's newest masterpiece danced in the soft breeze, glowing in the slight sliver of yellow moonlight.

Elena managed miniscule fits of sleep that left her more agitated than rested. Still, when the sun rose, Elena did as well. She tied the apron around her waist, preparing to brew coffee for herself and Daniel and make *arepas* for the children. When it was time, Elena walked into the yard to wake the children. Maribel stirred almost immediately, but Sammy didn't move. He lay there exactly as he had the night before. At first, Elena figured the poor child had worn himself out from playing with Maribel the day before, but once Maribel was up and dressed, and Daniel sat at the table with his coffee and Bible, Elena began to worry. To add to her concern, Elena noticed that Coco was more animated than ever. Maribel became increasingly uncomfortable, and Elena could see in her granddaughter's eyes a pleading mixed with apology.

When she could no longer endure her anxiety, Elena returned to the fort in the yard and made another attempt to wake Sammy. This time she gently shook him, but he did not stir or show any signs of consciousness. Moments later, both Daniel and Maribel followed her out as well. Together, the three of them made attempts to wake Sammy, but it was to no avail. Maribel broke into tears. Coco thrashed violently while Elena tried to calm her granddaughter, and Daniel cradled Sammy in his arms.

"Qué le pasa?" Elena begged, still holding Maribel close to her bosom as she sobbed and Coco swung desperately in every direction.

"He's breathing, but he won't wake up. We have to tell Beatriz immediately, Mama."

Elena looked up at the paper Sammy and paper Maribel, who still held hands. They stirred slightly, but now their little dance was solemn, a static movement back and forth rather than the jubilant and whimsical waltz from the night before.

CHAPTER 14

Deanna's Reckoning

"You fool. You should have come to see me much sooner, you know." Magdalena Huerta, *la curandera,* growled these first words the moment a frantic Deanna Fabo entered her home.

"I thought you were just a crazy old woman back then, but now ..."

"But now you understand, about the ghost, about the bad thing, about Beatriz."

"Yes," Deanna croaked, speaking between sobs.

"Well, I may be an old woman, even a crazy old woman at that, but it doesn't mean I don't know who people are and what becomes of those who play at magic they don't understand."

"Will he die? My grandson, Sammy, will he die?" Deanna leaned forward and pressed her hand to Magdalena's shoulder, as if through touch she, too, could conjure the future.

"That is mostly up to you and the other fools whose lies and nonsense have consumed these poor babies!"

"What do I do? Tell me, please, whatever it is, tell me, and I will do it! Even my own life I will give, but please, anything, anything!"

"All right, you foolish old woman, I know what I need from you. Tell me what you've done. Tell me everything."

CHAPTER 15

The Confession

"Beatriz's father, Manuel, left us when Beatriz was only two weeks old. She never knew her father. When Beatriz was pregnant with Sammy, her husband left, too. We are women abandoned, women left to raise our children alone. But we are strong women, we Fabos. We are a force to be reckoned with!

"When Beatriz was born, well, you can imagine... Even my own sisters, my own flesh and blood couldn't look at my *niña* Beatriz without wincing. She was so terribly, so pitifully homely. Through every stage of Beatriz's childhood, I kept hoping, I kept saying to myself and my sisters that she would grow out of this ugliness. I assured myself and others that this was God's plan. That God wanted Beatriz to be a humble girl, and that once tried and tested, he would grant her beauty and charm. But my poor Beatriz had neither.

"Oh, she was a very obedient child, who followed me around like a duckling follows its mother. Because other children were so cruel to her, I taught her to trust no one. I believed that I was protecting her. I told her she could trust only me. I didn't allow her any so-called friends, as I, having suffered my own fair share of cruelty and iniquity in life, could see through the riff-raff that attached themselves to Beatriz. You see, Doña Magdalena my sisters and I spoiled little Beatriz with the finest fabrics, the most beautiful silks and the richest tapestries and jewels. Beatriz was so desperate for friends, so lonely for company, she couldn't see through the malicious intentions of greedy and envious children who befriended her only to take advantage of her riches.

"Do you know how many children entered Beatriz's room in her early years only to steal from her, to take the very finest and most beautiful of her possessions? Oftentimes, stealing wasn't even necessary. You know my poor little Beatriz practically bribed children in return for their kindness? She gave away scarves and necklaces; she showered these little *pulgas* with gifts of expensive perfumes and patent leather shoes. But once the children got what they came for, where do you think that left Beatriz, eh? Same place as always. Rejected. Alone. The object of ridicule!

"Then *she* appeared. Carmen Trozco. Well, she wasn't a Trozco yet, no. She was just Carmen *la bella,* Carmen *la linda.* Yes, I knew from fellow patrons of the *panadería* that Carmen had been dealt a painful hand in life herself, but she was given the gift of beauty, and that beauty eventually lured a fine man like Daniel Trozco. Carmen was warm, too, *bien gracíosa.* Not like Beatriz—Beatriz who stared at her feet, who walked like a ghost! No, Carmen was blessed with this beauty and charm. Regardless of what cruel pangs she'd suffered in her past, she had the thing men chase and women envy.

"For some time, my sisters had been studying the Old Ways. Both aspired to be *curanderas,* mostly because they wanted to help Beatriz. It was my sister Soledad who discovered a spell, a beauty spell."

Magdalena Huerta scolded Deanna. "Well Señora Fabo, didn't I tell you? That you needed to fix the thing inside first? You foolish woman! I was born a *curandera.* You should have listened!"

"Don't you think I understand now? Let me finish, please, Magdalena. Please listen and take pity, if not on me, then have pity for Beatriz and Sammy, for Carmen and Maribel, for they are the ones I have caused to suffer!"

Deanna went quiet but her breathing still revealed rage.

"As I was saying, it was Soledad who found a *remedio.* We would have to steal beauty. Beatriz knew nothing of what we were doing. Nothing at all. I knew there was no other beauty greater than that of Carmen. Not in all my years had I ever seen a beauty that came close.

"I could tell that Beatriz felt warmly towards Carmen, and Carmen found Beatriz endearing. But how could I let my poor daughter take any more chances on promises of friendship or kindness? Especially since this time we would be the thieves. We would take what we wanted for our own good.

"Beatriz had given Carmen two beautiful silk flowers for her hair. It was then I saw the opportunity to steal Carmen's beauty. I visited Carmen shortly after and insisted the gift was a mistake, that Beatriz had given something that was not hers to give. It was with the strands of Carmen's hair closed inside the clip that Soledad worked the *remedio*.

"Everything was ready. We were going to take the beauty we stole for Beatriz, and her life would change forever. At that time, so much had been taken from all of us. Do you think I felt any pangs of guilt for what I'd done to Carmen Trozco? No, I did not. In those days, I felt that God owed me—owed *us*—and that we were simply claiming a gift He'd forgotten to grant us Himself.

"Soledad had begun mixing the ingredients, and we were so close."

Deanna shook her head and sighed.

"*Entonces? Qué?*" Magdalena urged.

"*No se,* Beatriz fell to the floor. She shook. She convulsed. *La pobresita!* And still she did not know what we had done. She knew only that her *tías* and her mama were trying to make her beautiful. But she did not know what price we had paid. Really, none of us did. Not until now."

"*Mira,* Deanna!" Magdalena said. "Gather your family. We are going to set things straight, you and me."

CHAPTER 16
The Healing

The healing would take place in the Trozco home. The children were to lie on the floor, Maribel on her side, both her hands holding Sammy's, and Coco outstretched in the other direction. Every member of the Trozco and Fabo families would sit in a circle surrounding the two pitiful children. They would each hold a lighted candle. They would hold back their tears and keep their hopes alive until the ceremony was complete.

But first, it was the *curandera,* Magdalena Huerta, who would address them all and explain:

"When you kill the spirit of a child, that spirit—which is supposed to inhabit the vessel of the child always—turns into something else, something darker. The ghost I saw in Beatriz so long ago was the other Beatriz. That is, that part of Beatriz made of the spirit, the spirit part of Beatriz that had loosened itself from her, so that it lived inside of her still, but now as a lost and fearful ghost. Do you wonder what broke Beatriz's spirit? Her loneliness! Her pain! The ridicule and torment from other children, even from adults. The endless and ridiculous concoctions that you, Deanna, and your foolish sisters searched for, trying to change the outside of Beatriz, which wasn't broken, but was just as it was meant to be, instead of healing the inside, which was crying out in pain! In agony!

"The spirit would need another home. So it waited to be born anew. When Sammy came along, it was to be reborn. The spirit and Sammy would become one. But because of the spell—that dangerous and hideous spell—Sammy was damned. The fates of Sammy and Maribel, the destinies of Beatriz and Carmen, intertwined. You had stolen Carmen's beauty, but the ghost inside Beatriz rejected it, just as I feared, just as I tried that day so many years ago to warn you. The broken spirit was siphoned into Carmen's womb, into Maribel. This is why Maribel is such a very, very special child. You see, she carries not only her spirit, but the spirit that was to be Beatriz's, and later Sammy's. Do you understand what I mean when I say spirit? I do not mean the soul. Beatriz and Sammy have their souls intact. The spirit is the magic, most greatly experienced when we are children. The spirit is at the core of who we are. It is our joy! It is our passion for life!

"When the broken spirit of Beatriz meant to be reborn in Sammy found herself in a strange home, inside Carmen and then in Maribel, it reached out. The spirit was so desperate and restless, so angry and confused that it tried with all its might to break out of Maribel. This breaking out is what *truly* killed that dear Carmen Trozco, not the sight of her child."

Could it be true? Elena gazed upon not just her granddaughter, but Coco, with new eyes. The idea of Spirit moving from one house of flesh to another remained abstract, impalpable. But the thought that Carmen had died not because she was mortified by her daughter's deformity, but as a consequence of Coco's desire to exist and be born anew into the world, left Elena with a transcendent gratitude for her own Spirit. She looked upon those souls who filled the room, those that she had scolded and refuted, and those she'd forgiven and even nurtured. For the first time in her life, she saw these men and women as more than flesh and blood, but as houses for spirits whose journeys were sometimes dark and tangled, but priceless and essential to joy.

"So where does the spirit go?" Magdalena continued. "Where does it dwell now? The spirit lives attached to Maribel, in the form of Coco. Remember, the spirit reached out. The spirit begged to return to its rightful home, but because beauty was stolen, a price had to be paid. The beauty that is Sammy—that unnatural, overwhelming beauty—was not a gift but a curse, because in return for beauty, the spell had cost the Fabo family the most important part of any human creature. It had cost them the spirit of a child and there is nothing more magical, more potent, or more powerful than that.

"Broken and in pain, this spirit lives in Maribel's third arm. Sammy lives like a parasite, only feeling truly alive in Maribel's presence, because in Maribel lives the spirit that was meant to be his, the spirit stolen for him, all for the petty and mundane gift of superficial beauty! What has beauty done for your grandson, Deanna? Hmm? *Mira lo qué has hecho! Maldíta!*

"And Daniel, do you not know how you came to fall in love with Beatriz so unexpectedly? How you look upon her as if she was an uncommon and indescribable beauty?"

This time Elena turned her attention towards her son, and to Beatriz. She thought of the many times Beatriz waited at the gate for Sammy after he'd spent the afternoon with Maribel. Not once had Elena invited Beatriz inside, not in all those years, never knowing that Beatriz was the object of her son's affection, never knowing that Beatriz might own Daniel's heart.

"You must sense something. No," Magdalena spoke to Daniel sternly, but without malice, "*Pues, te digo*: Love does not die with our bodies. Whatever kindness and love we leave behind when our bodies give out, it lives on. It is, the biggest part of what makes the spirit; it is the light. Carmen's light was very, very big, no? When Carmen passed, where did her spirit go? Her spirit could either move on to the other realm, or it could remain on this earth that God has given us. Carmen's light was so bright, and it had touched Beatriz so powerfully as a young girl, that when Carmen passed, what was left behind of that light lit the path to guide the spirit back. Little by little, year by year, that spirit has come to live in Beatriz. On the outside, Beatriz is still the woman you and others thought her to be. Her flesh hasn't changed. But the flesh is a weathered garment we all have to take off eventually. The spirit can last forever if and when we are careful. None of you have been careful! That is why these children have suffered!"

What could the Trozcos and Fabos say or do after such a damning speech, but bow their heads and sit in silence. For years, Daniel had kept his relationship with Beatriz Fabo a secret, a secret that both Sammy and Maribel carried on their small backs. For years, Elena had blamed Beatriz for cursing her family, when really, Beatriz had suffered a great deal more than Elena could have imagined. Deanna had kept her daughter from living in the world and finding her place in it. She had played with powerful magic she didn't understand and cursed two children at once, not to mention causing the death of the one soul who'd genuinely cared for her daughter, Beatriz: Carmen Trozco. And, if it weren't for Sammy's overwhelmingly tragic disposition, Dr. Matos might still be alive, too. When Magdalena could see that the families were deeply remorseful, she spoke to them again.

"Enough! This will not be about you any longer. It is time to now focus on these two children. We will pray first, and then it will begin."

"*Espíritu santo,*" they began, and before long, the Trozcos and Fabos formed a chorus of prayers and supplications that melded into one harmony, into one terrible and beautiful song.

While members of the two families prayed, Magdalena entered the circle and took her place on the floor next to the children—Sammy, the comatose angel, and Maribel, the scared but hopeful little girl dressed in red. Magdalena opened a small box made of cedar, and from that box she removed an orange and red silk flower and with a smile, she put it in Maribel's black hair. Then she looked over at Beatriz, and Beatriz nodded and came forward holding a pair of scissors. She took the scissors to her long, stringy grey and brown hair and handed a lock to Magdalena. Magdalena pulled a locket from under her blouse and from inside she retrieved a white stone that resembled a large molar. From inside the stone oozed a liquid, a perfume of sorts. She then turned her attention to Coco, who had to be restrained to avoid hurting herself or anyone else. In a gentle and purposeful gesture, Magdalena gathered Beatriz's hair in a ribbon and tied it three times and carefully pressed the lock of hair into Coco's palm. Finally, she poured the liquid out of the tiny tooth-like stone and spoke some words in a language that was neither Spanish nor English. They were words no one in the room had heard before, but somehow, everyone recognized their power. The melody of each and every person's singing went from chant to lullaby, and the whole room filled with the scent of the magic liquid so that it smelled like the forehead of a newborn baby, like the first day of summer, like the rain when it soaks fresh grass. It was the scent of rebirth.

It was then that Coco clenched her fist and Beatriz fainted.

"Coco," Maribel spoke. "My Coco ..."

Just as Elena started towards her, something even stranger occurred.

"*Mira!*" Magdalena announced.

Every paper creation Maribel had ever cut and folded and labored over, every work of art she'd poured her heart and imagination into cut loose from its strings as it came to life. Paper elephants and tigers, paper rabbits and turtles—even the paper Elena holding the paper Maribel stirred to life. The Fabos and Trozcos watched as the paper creatures exchanged animated expressions and fluttered from corner to corner, as if searching for a way out.

Magdalena opened the kitchen window overlooking the garden and the field. Elena helped her granddaughter off the floor and walked behind her towards the open window.

"It is time, Maribel. Say goodbye to Coco," Magdalena gently urged.

The farewell was the last thing needed to complete the healing, to allow the trapped spirit to complete its journey home to Sammy

Fabo. For Beatriz it would mean a release from the weight of a child's broken heart.

"Coco?" Maribel said, searching the walls and corners of her home while her paper dragons and cranes gathered around her. "Goodbye, Coco."

With that, all the animals, in all the colors of carefully folded paper freed themselves like a flock of birds. In a beautiful and breathtaking display, Maribel's menagerie flew out of the window and into the sky and then disappeared.

Coco had vanished. Sammy was awake, and something had changed in him. He was still beautiful, but now he was also whole, and that wholeness gave him a texture and a color he'd never had before.

Beatriz awoke after some urging, and when she sat up, her eyes filled with joyful tears as she was face-to-face with her newly reborn son.

"Mi hijo! Mi querido! Ven!" she cried, with her arms wide open. Sammy, wearing his brightest smile, rushed into his mother's arms. His heart beat so loudly, the rhythm filled the room with joy.

Elena held Maribel close, while Sammy, Beatriz and Daniel sobbed and smiled and, lastly, sang the final hymn to bring the healing to a close.

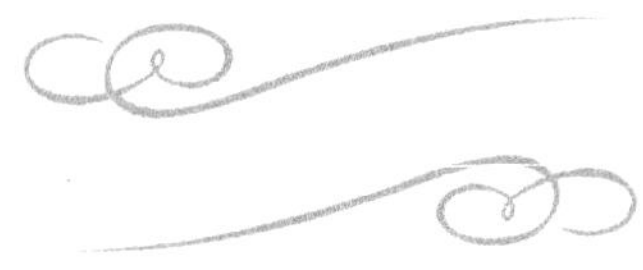

Chapter 17

The Wedding

Although Deanna offered to sew Beatriz's wedding dress, it was Elena's gift that Beatriz accepted. She would wear Carmen's wedding dress. After all, she carried Carmen's spirit, her love, her kindness and her light within her. Beatriz said she couldn't think of a better way to honor the one woman in her life who had offered sweetness when the rest of the world only offered pain.

Maribel debuted a brand new red dress, the first dress she'd ever worn that didn't need a third armhole. Sometimes she'd experience the phantom pain common when we lose something that has been a part of us for so long. But what she gained in return for her loss lifted her high above the skies of sadness or longing. She gained a mother in Beatriz, a brother in Sammy, and she could now experience the world with less weight on her back. In her hands, she carried a bouquet of baby's breath and pink carnations.

Daniel wore his hair slicked back. He pinned one of Maribel's paper roses to his lapel. In his vows, he told Beatriz how beautiful she was and how grateful he was to her for healing his heart and honoring Carmen's spirit. Sammy, dressed in a powder blue suit, his little face beaming with light, carried their rings on a satin pillow.

Elena and Deanna, who put aside their differences long enough to share the same pew at the front of the church, barely contained their tears, their joy and their relief. They had each gained a grandchild, and one of them had gained a son, and the other a daughter. With the help of Magdalena Huerta, who also attended the wedding, Elena and Deanna had also released their loved ones from the curse of secrecy, of envy, of blame.

Magdalena herself did not take a seat in one of the front pews, or any pew at all for that matter. Instead, she stood in the doorway of the church with the lilac-scented breeze at her back, leaning on her cane, her own spirit rising and dancing inside the walls of her body.

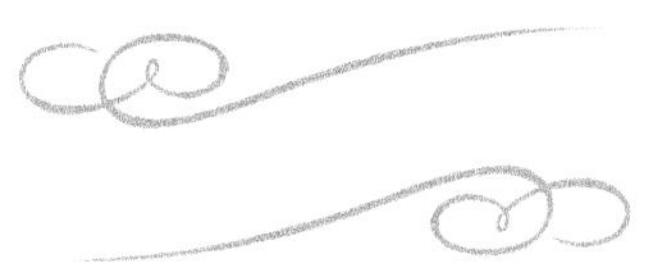

Chapter 18
Elena Sleeps

For the first time in her life—of how many years she'd lost count—Elena found herself alone. The solitude was both a relief and a sorrow. The aloneness allotted space for freedom, it championed inner peace, but it wasn't without holes: Maribel, Daniel and even Beatriz shaped holes.

For the first few days after the wedding, without her family, and without the paper creatures Elena had become so accustomed to, Elena wandered her home like a ghost. It occurred to her she might even be a ghost—that she was one of those spirits who clung to the earth, one of those poor, stupid souls who rattles chains and knocks on floorboards and wonders why no one can see or hear them. Had she really died? And if so, how could it be she did not see the light everlasting? Why had she been damned to an empty, lonely house? She had been after all a God-fearing woman, a mother who gave her best, her all, who toiled day and night, who was widowed in her prime. She'd loved her granddaughter as if they shared a heart.

Even the business with Beatriz had been rectified, and she felt it would be a very petty God indeed to punish her for a mistake she'd already paid for dearly in her living years. Beatriz had forgiven her.

The thoughts made Elena angry, so angry she walked through the house at a faster pace now, not the slow hum of a lonely ghost, but the gait of a woman filled with rage. She knocked down the potted plants in the windowsill and threw two pieces of her fine china set against the wall. She cried tears so hot they stung her face.

After her fit was over, Elena felt something she'd yearned for, for decades now. She felt the heaviness of tired eyelids, the surrender of sleep.

Before she fell to sleep, Elena said to herself, "Maybe now I will see the light."

Elena had only dozed off for a few minutes when a commotion came to her door. *Los ángeles,* she thought, *los ángeles me llevan al cielo!* But before she could stand on her own two feet, her home erupted with laughter and the scent of rich foods, the high-pitched squeals of two children. Her family had returned.

"Abuelita!" Maribel cried and ran to Elena with open arms and sweet kisses.

"Abuela!" Sammy joined in.

"Mama, we brought Sunday dinner," Daniel said, his arm proudly wrapped around his new wife's shoulders.

"*Buenos días,* Doña Elena." Beatriz greeted Elena with a kiss on each cheek.

That day, for the first time since becoming a mother, an *abuela,* Elena sat while her family toiled in the kitchen and served her. The grandchildren propped her feet on a stack of pillows, her son read from the Psalms, and Beatriz cleaned up the broken dishes, no questions asked.

After supper, the children spoiled her with kisses again, and Beatriz and Daniel stood on the patio, holding one another tight.

"Mari," Elena said, "Please, take Sammy and make me more of your *críaturas de papel, los extraño.*"

Maribel nodded excitedly, grabbed Sammy by the elbow, and off they went to gather supplies.

At peace in her rocking chair, where she'd once nursed Daniel and rocked Maribel to sleep, Elena was overcome with sleepiness again. But this time, it was delicious, and she felt not just her face but her whole body smiling. She was not a ghost, just an old and happy woman. When she closed her eyes, she did not find darkness or pain, she only saw the light.

THE END

About the Author

Kristy Webster is a writer, artist and mother of two. She earned her MFA in Creative Writing from Pacific Lutheran University and her Bachelor's Degree from the Evergreen State College where she majored in creative writing, visual arts, and feminist studies. Her work has appeared in several online journals such as: Lunch Ticket, Pithead Chapel, The Feminist Wire, Shark Reef Literary Magazine, Pacifica Literary Review, The Molotov Cocktail, Connotation Press and A Fly in Amber. Her work is also featured in two print anthologies by GirlChild Press, A Woman's Work and Just Like a Girl. She lives in Port Townsend, Washington with too many cats.

The Mason Key III
The Return
A John Mason Adventure
by David Folz

Mason and Marie fend off pirates en route to her father's plantation. John struggles with the Third Principle, Honor, and the Cruelty of Slavery while making his way back home.

Raw Man

by Pulitzer-Prize nominee Fred Rivera, winner at the 2015 International Latino Book Awards

This lightly-novelized Vietnam memoir, now required reading at major universities, derives its title from the author's epiphany: "Twenty-seven years after I got on the flight home, I saw that Nam war was just raw man spelled backwards. I'm pretty raw today."

Angus MacDream and the Roktopus Rogue
by Isabelle Freedman

Young adults on a mythical Scottish island save the world. Delightfully illustrated by Teri Rider.

The Wanderer
by Derek Thompson

A stranger wakes up on a deserted beach and embarks on a journey of discovery. The first in our *Magical Realism* series.

The Coffee Shop Chronicles, Vol. I,
Oh, the Places I Have Bean!

An anthology of award-winning stories inspired by events that occurred over a cup of coffee.

The Coffee Shop Chronicles, Vol. II,
A Jolt of Espresso

Stories condensed to exactly 100 words each,
inspired by our favorite brew.

Visiting Angels and Home Devils

by Dr. Don Hanley, Ph.D.

A discussion guide for couples.

The Courtesans of God

by Thornton Sully

A novel based on the real life of a temple priestess
in the palace of the King of Malaysia.

Bounce

by Pulitzer Prize winner Jonathan Freedman

A nutty watermelon man, a spurned she-lawyer, a
frustrated carioca journalist and a misanthropic
parrot set out to Brazil to change the world.

Left Unlatched
in the hopes that you'll come in…

A Book of Poetry by R.T. Sedgwick

Winner of the 2012 San Diego Book Awards – Poetry.

The Sky is Not the Limit

A Book of Poetry by R.T. Sedgwick

Our Award-Winning Poet follows through
with a volume of new work.

The Boy with a Torn Hat
by Thornton Sully

Debut novel was a finalist in the 2010 USA
Book Awards for Literary Fiction
"Henry Miller meets Bob Dylan in this coming of age romp played
out in the twisted alleyways and smoky beer halls of Heidelberg.
Sully is a cunning wordsmith and master of bringing music to
art and art to language. Excessive, expressive, lusty, and once in
a blue metaphor—profound. Here is what I mean: 'Some women
are imprisoned like a tongue in a bell—they swing violently but
unnoticed until the moment of contact with the bronze perimeter
of their existence—and thenthe sound they make astonishes us its
power and pain and beauty, and its immediacy' —Wunderbar"
—Jonathan Freedman, Pulitzer Prize winner

A Word with You, Vol. I
The Best from A Word with You Press

An anthology of select winners from the literary con-
tests of *A Word with You Press* from 2009 to 2015

Max and Cheez go to Spain
by Naureen Zaim and David Ulrich

A delightful illustrated children's book finds two cats on the first of
many adventures, stowing away in a suitcase to Spain. What other
countries will they investigate, now that they have the travel bug? A
great way to introduce young children to the cultures of the world.

Falling for France

by Nancy Milby

The first in *A Foreign Affair* series finds Annie Shaw having to choose between a successful career and real romance with a French aristocrat, and wanting both.

French Twist

by Nancy Milby

The saga continues as American archeologist Louise Marcel becomes entangled in nasty business on French soil, as she conceals her own hidden agenda.

Finding France

by Nancy Milby

The third in *A Foreign Affair* series finds Gabrielle Walker lamenting a life unraveling when a letter informs her she is the inheritor of a large estate in France. Then it gets complicated!

Finding Home

by Nancy Milby

Etienne, the recurring enigma in the series *A Foreign Affair*, is brutal to his enemies but a gentle giant to those he loves. Can the secret woman in his past enter his life again? Perhaps, but not with complications—some predictable, but some …

A Word with You Press
Publishers and Purveyors of Fine Stories in the Digital Age
310 East A Street
Suite B
Moscow, Idaho 83843